Sarah's Diary

Tshombe

T.S. AMEN PUBLISHING
Oakland, California

For information, please send written queries to:
T.S. Amen Publishing
490 Lake Park Ave, 10824
Oakland, CA 94610

Library of Congress Control Number: 2006910029

ISBN: 978-1-7321857-3-9

Printed in the United States of America
First Printing: March 2007
Release Date: July 2012

DEDICATION

This book is dedicated to the loving memory of my aunt, Claudette.
Her spirit is the lighthouse that continues to shine bright for us all to see.
We miss you.

ACKNOWLEDGMENTS

I would like to acknowledge all the individuals who have assisted me with this work. Thank you for your help. You know who you are.

INTRODUCTION

In life, there are always questions that cannot be explained and answers to questions not yet asked. The truth outside experience does not exist—only assumptions and judgments. For those who judge, I ask: How do you know the truth from a lie? For those who assume, I ask: Why believe something, if you're unsure. The truth is only for the participants of the experience. For the all the others, welcome...

THE DIARY

CHAPTER 1
Ericka & Alex

June 16, 1993

My first entry in my diary! I don't know what to say. My mother thought it would be a good idea to write down my feelings to help adjust to California since we just moved here. I guess I should 'cause I don't have anything else to do. Well, let me start off by saying that Southern California sucks and I miss my friends in Arizona. We have only been here for a week and I hate it! It's going to be a long and boring summer. I hope my friend Jenny can come out to visit for a little while, but I don't think she wants to. When I talked to her she said, "Sarah, what are we going to do in Burbank?" So I'm not sure if she is going to come. My dad said that it would be best if I did not go back and visit for a while so I can make a clean break from my old life. That's my dad! Teaching me through life experiences. I'm 14- years old. Visiting my friends is not going to hurt me. They treat me like such a kid! My brother gets whatever he wants, and he is only two years older than me. I'll bet he gets to go back and visit his girlfriend. Jason is their pride and joy! Tomorrow, my mom is taking us to the local high school to register and check out the campus. I wish I could just take home study, 'cause California kids are conceited and spoiled. I do not think I'm going to fit in. I hate this place so much! I wonder if John misses me?

June 20, 1993

My life is so screwed up! That skank Jenny is going out with John! I have not even been gone a whole month. She knows I love him! We were together for nine months. He was my first kiss! She is supposed to be my best friend! This is just great. If we had not moved here, none of this would ever have happened. I wish I was dead!

June 22, 1993

My dad asked me if I want to go visit my old friends because he said I look "depressed." I cannot believe he would ask me that when he knows what happened. I told him, "I don't have any friends!" He let Jason go back and see his girlfriend. I think the only reason he offered was because my brother was already going back. My life is so messed up. I hate this place!

June 29, 1993

I met this girl named Ericka yesterday. She lives a few houses down. She is really cool! We are supposed to go out with some of her friends tonight. She is 16, which is cool 'cause she can drive. Her parents gave her a Porsche. California is crazy!

She smokes cigarettes and goes to my school. I really like her! Well, I have to get ready for tonight. Gotta go!

July 1, 1993

This has got to be the coolest place ever. I take back everything I said about California. Last night Ericka took me to a club in Hollywood (21 and over). All her friends have older IDs from their sisters or their friends. This girl named Tiffany, one of Ericka's friends, had an ID that looked like me so I could get in the club. Ericka was teaching me the names of cool drinks like cosmopolitans, Cape Cods, screwdrivers, and Long Islands. I smoked weed for the first time and was so drunk I barely remember anything. When I woke up we were at some dude's apartment in Hollywood and I didn't have my pants on. I was so scared 'cause I thought something had happened, but Ericka told me I threw up on my pants and she had washed them for me. She is so cool! The dude whose apartment we were at is Ericka's boyfriend. He is 24 and his name is Alex. He must have a rich family or something, 'cause when I asked him what he did for a living, he laughed and said I must not be from around here. We smoked more weed and ate breakfast, and then went back to Ericka's house and I called my mom, who could have cared less what I was doing. I told her I'd be home for dinner, got off the phone, and passed out!

July 5, 1993

Last night was so cool! We went to Six Flags and watched the fireworks and listened to some band playing heavy metal. Ericka snuck in a bottle of Bacardi rum and we were so wasted I don't know how we got to Alex's apartment. I think something happened 'cause I was real sore when I woke up, and I think I remember Alex and Ericka touching me. I think Alex sells drugs 'cause he has way too much stuff to just be smoking. What's really crazy is that a few other girls live there. I was so happy to get home and clean myself! When I got out of the car, Ericka hugged me, kissed me on the lips and told me to call her tomorrow. The strange thing is I did not mind the kiss! What's going on with me?

July 12, 1993

My father and I got into an argument today about me spending so much time with Ericka or in my room. I'm sorry if I don't fit into this perfect family, but what do they expect me to do-- sit and watch TV with them and tell them about my day? My dad said that I look like crap ever since I've been hanging around *that girl*, and that my attitude has changed. Maybe I just woke up to what bullshit this world is all about. I'm locked in my room with a bottle of gin and a pack of cigarettes. I'm not even mad at the old bastard anymore. It's not his fault he does not understand!! UP IN SMOKE!!

July 20, 1993

I tried crystal today and am so wired right now I can't stop shaking. It was weird because Alex called me up and asked me to watch his apartment for him while he ran some errands. He took out a package and put it into a drink of rum and coke, and then he told me to drink it so I would stay alert. He fired up a joint and left a few joints for me to smoke while he was gone. Here's the weird part: he told me not to open the door to any men, but if women came, to let them in and tell them he will be back in a few hours. The first girl that came was dressed in a miniskirt and high heels, and she was driving a Mercedes; her name was Candy. She had an envelope for Alex—it was full of credit cards. She spoke with me for a minute about where I was from. She told me she just came back from Arizona. The next girl who came was dressed like a teenager, with baggy pants on. Her name was April and she had a suitcase for Alex. She drove a convertible classic Mustang. She had an accent like she was from Italy. Two more girls came together named Peaches and Kelly. They looked like secretaries. I don't know what they had for Alex. We sat drinking for a while, then Alex showed up with Ericka, and they had more money than I've ever seen in my life.

Ericka told me it was over 80 grand! When I asked her how she got it, she snapped at me and said, "Don't ask questions like that." I wanted to stay, but she took me home. I guess she is mad at me for asking dumb questions.

August 3, 1993

Ericka gave me some jewelry to hide in my room today. She said it was her grandmother's jewelry and she needed a place to keep it, but it sure is a lot of jewelry for one person to have. Why can't she keep it at her house? She told me that she is going to come over tonight so she can spend the night. I told her it would be cool. She looks like she has been up for a couple of days. What's going on?

August 4, 1993

Ericka just left. I feel wired 'cause she kept touching me. She told me that she loved me and that she was going to leave Alex. I'm just glad we got drunk first. I did not like it. She also left a gun here. She said she already had one at her house, but she needed to leave one here for a little while. I told her I can hold the jewelry, but guns are out of the question, so hurry up and get it. I think that upset her, 'cause she got quiet and left. Why does she need a gun?

August 11, 1993

I have not seen Ericka for a week. She has not been home and has not returned my calls. I called Alex, and he said if I heard from her to tell her he is looking for her too, and he hung up after he said that. What is she doing? I hope she is all right. I think I'm going to stop hanging out with her, 'cause she seems like bad news.

August 13, 1993

Ericka just showed up at my house tonight saying she needed to talk to me. I was totally mad because she just shows up out of the blue and she was drunk. She kept talking about a Blue Man who was coming to get her, and when I asked her where she had been, she told me she went camping, and when I asked her where, she said, "With the Blue Man," and started laughing. When I told her Alex was looking for her, she said, "My brother has always been a worrier." When I said, "Your brother?!" she straightened up her laughing demeanor and got serious. Then she said she needed the gun and jewelry. I gave it to her, and she left in a hurry. All she said was thanks—no good-bye, no see you later—and she had a strange look on her face like she just got some shocking news. She seems real weird to me now. It's almost like I don't even know her. I wonder what she meant by

"My brother has always been a worrier?" Is Alex her brother? I've seen them kiss before! Something is real strange.

August 28, 1993

I have not seen or heard from Ericka since she picked up her stuff. I have been hanging out with my family and this girl named Heather. Heather is cool, and she is my age. She drinks a lot, and I mean all the time, but it's cool 'cause she doesn't look drunk. She reminds me of Ericka. They are both so pretty with the brown hair, brown eyes, California tans, and perfect teeth with hourglass bodies. Heather doesn't take me to clubs— she likes to go out at night and drink in the parks. She really likes to hear about my friends from Arizona and what it was like there. It's good to have somebody just to talk to.

September 7, 1993

My first day of school was crazy. Ericka doesn't even go to my school. I was looking all over for her, and nobody even seems to know her. I told Heather about it, and she said that Ericka is probably taking home study this year. I tried to call her, but her cell phone is disconnected. I tried to call Alex, but he has not been home. I was really hoping she was going to be at school with me. I like my classes and my teachers. Heather has two classes with me, and to my surprise, I like a lot of the other kids. They are not all conceited and stuck-up. I went by Ericka's house today, but nobody is ever home. I haven't seen or heard from her since she got her stuff. She must be with Alex.

September 9, 1993

When I came home today, the police were at Ericka's house, and there were ambulances. I went to see what was wrong, and a police officer was putting the yellow tape around the house. A guy in the crowd told me that this was a homicide investigation. When I asked him if a girl my age was found he said, "Yes, two of them." I can't believe Ericka is dead. I asked about her parents and he said, "There were no adults in there." I wonder who that other girl was? This is crazy!

September 10, 1993

I went to Alex's apartment today and the place was empty! What the hell is going on? I've got to find out what is going on. Did Alex have something to do with it? Was he Ericka's brother or her boyfriend? Who is the Blue Man she was talking about? This whole thing is driving me crazy. Last night Heather and I got drunk, and I started crying 'cause Ericka was a really cool person and this shouldn't have happened to her. Then Heather said, "Yeah, her and her sister were so quiet and never bothered anybody." I was like, "Her sister?" She said,

"Yeah, her twin sister, Monica." "Ericka never told me she had a twin sister!" Then Heather told me she can't understand that because they were always together and did not have many friends. See what I mean by this is driving me crazy? So I stayed home from school and went to Alex's apartment, and the place was like a ghost town. A neighbor told me that they must have left at night. He didn't see them leave. This whole thing is getting stranger by the minute. My dad just came in and told me they found Ericka's parents buried in the backyard, and it seems that the whole family had been dead for quite some time. He also said all of their jewelry and credit cards were taken. It looks like they were robbed, he said. Who would do this to them?

September 11, 1993

My mom said I could do home study this semester. I thought that was really cool, 'cause I am freaked out about Ericka. All the time I knew her, I never saw her parents or sister, and Heather said they were close and did not have many friends. I just can't understand that 'cause Ericka was so cool and she had a whole bunch of older friends. When I went back to her house after that first night out, she told me her parents were out of town, but she never mentioned a sister . . . why? So many unanswered questions. I asked her next-door neighbor had he ever seen Ericka's boyfriend, and he said to his knowledge the twins did not have any boyfriends—in fact, they did not have many girlfriends who came by regularly. He said that their father was real strict and that the girls were bookworms. I asked him did they have a brother, and he said in the 20 years he lived there—and he knew the family—he never saw a brother. So I guess Alex was her boyfriend and all that brother talk was because she was drunk. Where did Alex go? Who were those girls—Candy, April, Peaches, and Kelly? Why did Ericka and Alex have so much money? These questions are bothering me day in and day out. I need to go get Heather and have a drink. I hope I don't get in trouble.

September 13, 1993

It's late at night—3:22 a.m. to be exact! Every time I go to sleep, Ericka is in my dream. I just woke up from the worst one. Alex was strangling Ericka, and I was tied up. I couldn't move. She kept calling my name to help her, but I couldn't do anything. Then her twin sister Monica came running toward me with a knife. I don't understand what that could mean. The night before I dreamt I was at Ericka's house, but Ericka was not with me—I was all alone. So I began to look for her. When I looked outside to the backyard, there she was, so I ran toward her.

As I got closer, I could see she was busy her back was to me. I was calling her name as I was running, and finally she turned around. She had a shovel in her hand, and lying on the ground were her parents. Right now I'm scared to go to sleep. I don't want to dream about her anymore. What bothers me most is that my dreams of her are so twisted. Why can't I dream about us having fun or just hanging out? God, I wish they would find someone responsible for this so I could rest my mind. Maybe I should tell the police about Alex and the other girls, plus the money and the jewelry? I don't think she was serious about the Blue Man—I mean, how could a man be blue? Yeah, first thing in the morning I'm going down to the police station and tell them everything I know. Maybe then I'll be able to rest at night.

September 13, 1993

I am so freaked out right now. I went down to the police station to tell them everything I know. I gave them a description of Alex, and they had me look at mug shots. I was almost ready to give up when I saw his picture. I ID'ed him, and they ran a check on him. They came back and told me he died last year in a car accident—his picture shouldn't even be in there. I'm positive it was him. He had the same dark brown hair and eyes. He even had the diagonal inch-long scar above his eyebrow, and the big Greek nose and full mouth. The police were like, "Sorry, he's dead and has been dead for over a year. He couldn't have committed these murders." They wanted me to look through mug shots of women, but I was too freaked out, so I went home. I told Heather about it, and she said maybe I have just been up too long, but I'm positive that it was him. I have to get some sleep. This is way too crazy.

CHAPTER 2
Mom & Dad

September 14, 1993

My life is upside down. My brother doesn't care about me. He has a new friend named Erick and he gives me the creeps. He looks like Alex and his name is one letter off from Ericka. Jason woke me up yesterday evening and accused me of going in his room. "What the hell is wrong with you?" I said. "What the hell would I want in your room but some rats? Close my door and get out." That creepy dude Erick pulled him out, shut my door, and said, "Sorry." Is that not the worst thing Jason could do, when he knows my friend and her family were just murdered? I am pissed! I've got to do some of this homework, 'cause it's piling up on me. I think I'll call Heather to come help me.

September 16, 1993

My birthday is 10 days away. My parents are going out of town on my birthday. They wanted me to go with them, but I don't want to go to my uncle's house for my birthday. I decided to just chill here with Heather, get sloppy drunk and pass out. Heather wants to throw a party, but I don't like the idea of having a bunch of strangers in my house. It's not like they're coming to cheer me up or wish me happy birthday. All they're gonna wanna do is trash my house. Jason is probably going to have his friends over. It's amazing how fast he can become the most popular guy around. The phone is always ringing for him, and he already has a few girls that seem to be head over heels in love with him. I'm positive he is going to throw a party, 'cause that's the cool thing to do. I think I will take Heather to the park and stay out of Jason's way. That creepy dude Erick is always with him, and he always tries to talk to me when he sees me. Yesterday, he asked me if I wanted to go to the bowling alley with him and his friends. I told him, "No thank you," and then he said, "I heard about your friend and I'm sorry to hear that. I knew her and her sister—they were cool people. If you'd like to hang out sometimes, I'd be glad to show you around." I told him, "Thanks, I'll keep that in mind." Maybe I should be a little nicer to him. He is not such a bad guy, plus he's kind of cute, but he's Jason's friend, so I don't know. I've got to go 'cause Heather is here; we're going to the mall. Big sales. Shopping. Shopping. Shopping!

September 17, 1993

Heather is crazy. We shoplifted some clothes from the mall—it was totally awesome! We tried on clothes, then put on our old clothes on over them and just walked out. Then Heather returned some clothes she had stolen for cash back! She got like

20

six hundred dollars, and bought some weed and drinks. She said she does it so her parents won't think she spends the money they give her on drugs. Then she told me a story about how she got busted by her parents with some weed while she was already drunk. In the middle of denying she was drunk, she threw up everywhere. It was hilarious. She is so crazy. I love her! We went to the park and got wasted. We were singing and dancing to our own tunes. I haven't had that much fun in a long time. We went to the pizza parlor afterward and ordered a pizza. While we were waiting for our order, my brother and that dude Erick came in. I was scared at first. I didn't want him to tell my parents I was high, but he was so baked out of his mind that he was probably more scared of me telling than I was of him. Erick said something like, "It must run in the family," and we all broke out laughing. We hung out eating pizza. I started talking to Erick. I told him I wouldn't mind going out with him if Jason wasn't there. He understood and said Jason doesn't have to come. So me and Erick are going to the bowling alley this weekend. I'm kind of excited. He is hella cute! Those big brown eyes he has. Oh my god, I like one of my brother's friends! I have got to call Heather.

Me and Erick went out to the bowling alley tonight. We were having a lot of fun, and then things got crazy again. Erick's sister came over to where we were sitting. I looked up in shock. It was that girl Candy who had been at Alex's house. When I called her Candy, she looked at me like I was crazy. I'm like, "You don't remember me? I'm Ericka's friend! I was watching Alex's house for him and we talked about how you had just come back from Arizona." She had the same look on her face when she said, "You must have me confused with someone else. My name is Michelle, and I have never been to Arizona." I was so stuck I didn't know what to do. I told her, "I'm sorry. I must have you mixed up with someone else." Then I went outside to smoke a cigarette. I'm thinking how that encounter was weird and embarrassing at the same time. I'm smoking and thinking that I'm positive that was her. But here's where it got confirmed: I see Peaches and Kelley in April's Mustang. They stopped, looked at me, laughed and then they took off. I ran inside and told Erick I felt sick and wanted to go home. His sister was gone! He sat quiet in the car for a long time. I was still shaking when he said, "My sister goes to school in New York. She just came into town tonight and my parents told her where I was. I'm sorry about that." I was like, "Yeah, it's cool.

I'm just kinda sick because that whole thing reminded me of Ericka. It's not your fault." He asked me if he could make it up to me with a movie and I told him yeah. I asked Heather if she knew Erick's sister. She said yeah, and I asked if his sister knows Ericka or her family? And she said no. Heather said I was drunk and confusing her with the other girl. When I told her about the Mustang, she asked me if I made eye contact. I was scared to say the truth. I told her it was dark! She was like, "You need to relax." But I know what I saw and I'm not crazy! Nobody believes me.

September 26, 1993 — My Birthday!

Last night my family had a small birthday party for me because my parents had to leave this morning for my uncle's house. It was cool for a cake and ice cream family party, but my mind kept wandering to the circumstances behind Ericka's death. I kept wondering if my family was safe, since whoever murdered Ericka and her family is still loose on the streets. Did the people who killed her ever see us together? That's a really scary thought. I sleep with a kitchen knife under my pillow and every little noise scares me. My mom and dad think I should see a counselor. I think they are right. It seems like I will not be enjoying this birthday, but I hope I do because I could use a happy day. Heather is coming over with a few movies and we are going to chill here. She's going to braid my hair. Well, I have to go take a shower and get ready for tonight. Happy birthday to me. Happy birthday.......happy birthday?

September 27, 1993

I don't have any more tears to cry. I can't believe what is happening. This is so crazy! What did I do to deserve all this? My uncle called last night and asked to speak with my dad. I was like, "Why did they leave?" and he said, "Leave? They never came here." A tingling sensation went all over my body like I was standing at the top of a 100-story building about to fall off. My voice was gone. I was out of breath from my heart beating so fast. I couldn't speak for what seemed like hours. My uncle was saying something like, "Calm down. Everything is going to be fine. They probably just stayed at a hotel or something." But I knew I would never see my parents alive again. My uncle is here right now and my aunt is at home in case they show up. The police were here at seven this morning filling out a missing persons report. I told them what happened to Ericka's family and the cops tell me they doubt it's related but they will look into it. Why is this happening to me? I'm so tired from crying all night. I need some sleep. I just want to go to sleep and wake up and have my parents home. I've got to go!

It's 8:00 p.m. and I just woke up. I feel sick and I really can't believe that this is happening. My brother told me that Heather called to see if I was OK. She is really a good friend. My uncle told me just now that there is still no word on the car or any sightings of my parents. I just can't believe all of this is happening. Why did we have to move here? If it's the same person who murdered Ericka, then am I next? Why were my parents murdered? OK, I have to get hold of myself and think positive: maybe they have been kidnapped for some type of ransom or information? They could still be alive! I'm just thinking negatively because of what happened to Ericka. They may have crashed in the mountains or the hills and be trapped or unconscious waiting to be rescued. It's only been a day and a half since they left, so there is still plenty of hope. Plus my dad is strong, so if someone tried to attack him and my mom, he would defend them and they would get away. Yeah, I have to think positive! I'm going to go downstairs and be positive and hopeful with my family.

September 28, 1993

Last night we had so much hope. We were remembering old times with Mom and Dad. We watched old home movies—all of us having good times. When I started to cry Jason put his arm around me and said they'll be home soon. I felt so secure and positive when I went to bed. This morning when I woke up, my aunt was here. I knew something was wrong. My uncle sat me and my brother down. He told us that the police found the car and my parents were not in it! I was happy 'til he told me this morning someone calling himself Richard called the house saying that we would never find the bodies and that they were both dead! The police said it may just be a prank, but they are going to put a tap and trace on the phone and put an officer at the house. They are checking the car for evidence and clues and will keep us posted. I'm in shock right now. I can't eat and I am having a hard time being positive. I don't feel safe going outside and I don't feel like talking to anyone right now. Why is this happening? I just wanna stay locked in my room forever and never come out. There is no positive explanation for all of this. I have to go—I don't feel good right now. I'm sick! This is all so sick.

     6:30 p.m. I keep seeing my parents' faces in my mind and they are always smiling at me. I wonder if it's a sign or if it's really them talking to me. Whatever it is, it does not make me feel good at all. I was upstairs in my parents' room this afternoon, just lying in their bed looking at our family photo album. I already miss them so much. I'm hurting so bad! What is going to happen to me and my brother? I don't wanna live with my aunt and uncle. Well, I guess it wouldn't be so bad at my uncle's house—it's really big, so they won't be in my face all the time. Plus my uncle Harry looks more like and acts more like my dad than any of their other brothers. Man oh man, I hope Pasadena is safer than Burbank. I don't even know why I am assuming he is going to take us in—he might not want any more kids living with him now that my cousins are grown up. It's my uncle's fault that we're out here in the first place. He talked my dad into coming here to work for his company. He said how good it would be for me and my brother to go to school out here. I'm scared! I feel abandoned and lost! If he doesn't want us, I will never talk to him again. I'm going to talk to him tomorrow about this. I have to know what I'm going to do. If there's one thing my dad taught me, it's was never to let unexpected events in life stop me from moving forward. "Life is about progress," he always used to say. I will keep moving forward, Daddy, and I will find out what really happened to you and mom if it's the last thing I do.

September 29, 1993

My uncle said that he would not have it any other way than for me and Jason to live with him and my aunt. I'm so happy. I don't feel so abandoned. They are still waiting on the guy calling himself Richard to call back. The police said if he doesn't call back by October 1st, then they are going to look in other areas—which, in other words, means that they are going to call it quits. Well, I have to go down to the station with my uncle to claim the property my parents left in the car. This is only the second time I have set foot outside my parent's house since my birthday and I am a little bit scared. What if they don't find them?

4:00 p.m. We just got back, and now I am more concerned than ever. All my parents' things were still in the car, including my mom's purse and my dad's wallet, which is very strange because my dad keeps his wallet in his pocket. The windows and tires were all intact and the keys were still in the ignition, a full tank of gas, and the car was in fine running condition. The police said it's like they just vanished into thin air. They searched the area where the car was found. The cops don't think they were kidnapped because the car was found in the parking lot of the always busy 24-hour K-Mart and no one reported any strange activity. There would have been a lot of screaming and a struggle would have taken place if my parents were taken against their will, and this particular store has parking lot security, so it would have been noticed. The police said they have received the security tapes and the tapes are under review. They should know something by tomorrow. This does not make any type of sense. Why would my parents get out of the car and leave their stuff in the car with the keys in the ignition, at K-Mart of all places? My mom wouldn't stop at K-Mart if it was the last place on earth. How did somebody get them out of the car without a struggle? Where did they really stop the car? Someone has got to know something, and the police don't seem to know anything. That's interesting.

September 30, 1993

The detectives came here this morning to ask me and my brother some questions. It upset me a lot because they were asking me things like, "When was the last time your brother got into an argument with your parents?" "How would you describe the relationship between your brother and your parents?" They did this for over an hour, and finally I had had enough and demanded a reason for this line of questioning because my brother would not have done anything like that to my parents. The detective said, "We have received information that your brother was at the store where your parents' car was found. The same night of the disappearance." I told the detective he had the wrong information. He said, "We may, but it is our job to investigate all legitimate information, and we are going to have to take your brother downtown for more questioning." That was four hours ago. My uncle went down to the station with a lawyer to get my brother an hour ago. I'm confused and upset about this whole situation. It's like something is trying to destroy everyone that is in my life. I'm so afraid right now. I just don't know what to do. Why is this happening to me? I have got to call my uncle and find out what's going on with my brother. I wanted to go to the station but my uncle told me it would be best if I stayed home with my aunt in case that guy called—plus, I was too upset to remain calm, he said. I hope everything is going to be all right. My uncle's car just pulled up. I've got to find out what's going on!

     5:45 p.m. I am so happy that the police did not arrest my brother and that he is safe at home with us. When I saw him getting out of the car with my uncle, I started crying and ran to him, held him, and did not want to let him go. He wasn't as happy to see me as I was to see him. I guess he is mad at being accused of killing his own parents. I can understand his anger. He went straight to his room and then he left about an hour ago. He said he needed to take a walk. I feel bad for him. After all that has happened, he gets accused of this? There is a killer on the loose. It is probably the same person who murdered Ericka and her family, and the police have no idea where to look, so they accuse my brother? My uncle told me of the things the police found out so far and it is really strange stuff. They told my uncle that half an hour before the car pulled into the parking lot, a person fitting the description of my brother pulled up with two females and one male. They stood by their car for a while, then the two females went into the store and purchased garbage bags and fertilizer. While they were in the store, my parents' car pulled up and a hooded individual got out of their car and spoke with the individual fitting my brother's description. Then the hooded individual walked off. When the two females came back, the original group left, but not before they stopped to talk with the hooded individual. I can't begin to explain how scared I am. This information has sent shock waves through my body. My uncle said he saw the video and that the image was poor quality. He said that he could barely make out clear pictures, because it was still-frame surveillance, but the kid in the picture did look like my brother. That's deep.

Why would so many people be in on killing my parents? Were they all in on it, or were they just being friendly to a killer? I wish I had a face to put with the killer so I would know what to look for. I don't even know what to look for, neither do the police, and that's what scares me. Well, I have to go eat dinner. I don't know if I can eat, but it can't hurt to try. Mom and Dad, wherever you are, I am going make sure everything is finished and taken care of for you. Miss you. Gotta eat.

[**Note to reader**: *The events Sarah spoke of on video were discounted by authorities. Her parents' car was found abandoned in the Hollywood hills.*]

October 1, 1993

The police decided to leave the tap on the phone for another week. Jason is still upset and does not want to come out of his room to socialize while they're here. My uncle is arranging for us to move in with him and my aunt. My mom's brother, my Uncle Fred, just found out and he wants us to live with him in Chicago. My grandparents are flying in from Arizona tomorrow to help out with things. My uncle tried to talk them out of it but they would not hear it. They said family is supposed to be together at times like this.

I sort of feel bad for my Uncle Fred because my mom was all the family he had left. My mom's parents died in a plane crash when my mom was still a teenager, and my uncle took care of her until she went off to college and met my dad. So I know he is heartbroken, but I just don't want to live with him in Chicago. But I told him we will think about it. I tried to talk to Jason about it, but he doesn't feel like talking. When I knocked on his door, he told me he was trying to sleep, go away. My uncle told me to wait until he is ready to talk. I feel bad for him. Oh my god, Heather is here! I have not seen her in so long. I've got to go.

October 2, 1993

It was really good to see Heather. I had not seen her since the night my parents disappeared. I told her all the stuff the police had found out, and then I told her that we were going to be moving to my uncle's house soon. She started to cry and told me that she wished she could do something to help. Then she started apologizing for crying. She said she wanted to be strong for me. Then she pulled out some Jim Beam and we got a little buzz, and that felt really good. She only stayed for two hours, but it was the best two hours I have had in a long time.

My grandparents came this morning and I had not seen them in so long. My dad and grandpa did not get along very well. We didn't visit them very much, but Grandpa Joe and Grandma Margaret always sent money on our birthdays and Christmas. I can tell that they are in denial 'cause they are talking like Mom and Dad are going to walk through the front door any minute. I guess they can't believe or understand how something like this could happen to innocent people. If Ericka's family had not been murdered, I guess I would still be in disbelief myself, but I know that the same person who murdered her family killed my parents. I don't know why this has to happen or who is next, but I intend to do something about it. I don't know what I'm going to do, but I'm going to do something.

I have to go downstairs and talk with my grandparents. Will write more later.

October 3, 1993

My Uncle Harry came in and told me to pack my clothes. He is taking us away from here today. I kinda don't wanna go because it's going to really feel like my parents are dead when I leave here. I'm starting to feel the pain of the first day all over again, but I have to be strong for my family. I have to finish packing!

October 4, 1993

Well, I'm at my uncle's house and I feel homesick already, but I guess this is my new home so I have to get used to it. Jason didn't even unpack last night—he just went to Erick's house as soon as we got here. Erick was outside already waiting for him. I'll have to watch him. I guess this is his way of dealing with it. Maybe he has the right idea? I should call Heather and see if she wants to come over to help me unpack. Yeah, I'm going to call her! Need some girl time.

6:45 p.m. Freaked Out! Heather is coming over tomorrow, but Jason came home and told me he had to show me something. He called me to his room and showed me Dad's wedding ring. He said that it was lying in the garage at the old house and he was scared to say something about it because of the police. He gave it to me, and then his friend Erick pulled up outside and he left again.

What is going on with Jason? Dad always had his ring on and it was a tight fit. It would have had to be pried off his finger. How did it just come off in the garage? This whole thing is really creeping me out. Jason has been acting really, really weird lately. The cops have a video of someone who looks like him in the parking lot talking to my parents' killer with garbage bags and fertilizer in his car. Now he hands me my dad's ring and says he found it in the garage? I wonder about him now! Could he have had something to do with our parents' disappearance? It just does not make any sense that he would do something like this—what should I do? I just can't deal with these thoughts in my head. I have to finish unpacking.

[**Note to reader**: *This ring has never been found. It is presumed to be with Sarah.*]

October 5, 1993

3:00 a.m. I just had a nightmare that Jason was in my room standing over me with blood on his face and a skull in his hand with blood on it. All I could do was look up at him. I couldn't move! I wonder what it means? It felt so real that I had to check my floor for blood drops. This is crazy! I have to go talk to him.

Well, he isn't in his room and he still has not unpacked — this is crazy. I have got to talk to him about this so I can clear my head of these crazy thoughts! I would hate for something to happen to him.

October 6, 1993

I totally forgot that Heather was coming over yesterday. My mind was so consumed with my parents, Ericka, and Jason, that when she showed up I was in shock to see her. It was good to see her and to talk to somebody about what's going on. I asked her what she knew about Erick and his sister. She told me that they have lived in Burbank for as long as she can remember and that they are pretty normal. Then she said she saw Erick and Jason last night coming from Old Man McKinley's house. I was like, "Who is that?" She told me she does not know much about him, but they call him the Blue Man because the color of his skin has a silvery-blue tint. I was like, "The Blue Man is who Ericka said was going to kill her, and she said she went camping with him." Heather told me it's impossible for Mr. McKinley to kill anyone because he is in a wheelchair. "Why would Jason and Erick go to Old Man McKinley's?" I said. Heather told me she did not know. I told her I need her help to find my parents' killer, and she said she would help me. We decided to investigate this Old Man McKinley first. She said she knows an old lady who lives on his street named Mrs. Finch. Heather's going to drop by and say hi to find out what Mrs. Finch knows about Old Man McKinley. My job is to find out what Jason is doing. Heather is coming over tomorrow, and we are going to swap information and plan from there. Well, I have to go and check out Jason's room. I don't want to fink on my brother to the cops but if he's hooked up with a group who hurt my parents then I'm going to have to do what I have to do. Gotta go before he gets home.

5:45 p.m. Jason came home five minutes ago and almost caught me coming out of his room. That was so close! I did not find anything that says he had anything to do with my parents' disappearance, but I did find some money—about $8,000! I wonder where he got all that money from and what he needs it for. Is that what he and Erick are into? We have everything we need—it's not like we're poor. Why would he need so much money? Mom and Dad always gave him money and clothes. Uncle Harry is rich and money is nothing to him. I have to go to dinner!

6:45 p.m. Jason asked if he could eat dinner in his room and wanted to be excused from the dinner table. Of course my uncle let him. I told my uncle to talk to him and he said that he will, but he wants to wait until Jason has had a little more time to cope with this whole situation. Before I could respond, he told me that the police have had no leads and are basically at a dead end. So it looks as if they are scaling back their investigation. I wonder if my parents will ever be found? It's just me and Heather looking for answers. I know what to do! My uncle said that the police are changing it from a missing persons to a homicide investigation. Uncle Harry said that they don't normally do that without the right information, but he has some friends in Burbank that helped him with it—so the case will never be closed! I guess that is a good thing but it feels kinda unsatisfying. We don't have any answers; all we have are too many questions. I am 15 years old. I should be dating boys and hanging out with friends, not worrying about my parents' and my friend's killer. I have to do some homework. I won't let changes in my life hold me down. I'll find a way to make this better.

October 7, 1993

Heather called and said she is not coming over, but she is onto something big. She said she spoke with Mrs. Finch and will tell me more later. I just wish she would hurry up. This is driving me crazy!

38

October 9, 1993

Heather came over yesterday with pictures of Old Man McKinley. The pictures freaked me out. He looks like an alien or something. I have never seen a human being with that color skin before. Anyway, Heather said she spoke with Mrs. Finch about Old Man McKinley. Mrs. Finch said that Mr. McKinley is anemic and that he needs blood all the time. She also said that Old Man McKinley used to be a janitor at our school 20 years ago but he was fired for telling kids that he could read their minds. There was a big scandal over it because the kids believed that Old Man McKinley was some sort of savior. The kids were all brainwashed and were brainwashing other kids into believing it. Mrs. Finch said the school found out that he was friends with some gypsies who were involved in some robberies, but the police could never charge him with anything.

Mrs. Finch said that Old Man McKinley does not talk to or associate with any of his neighbors, he has no kids and has never been married. She said that he rarely ever comes out of the house anymore and if he does it's at night. She said he is really weird and nobody wants to go near him. This is so strange to me because I cannot understand why Jason would be over there. I know he does not believe in saviors or anything like that. What would any of this have to do with murdering my parents or Ericka's family? A savior is here to save people. I have got to find out what is going on with Jason. Why was Ericka with this Blue Man? Why would he want to kill her and her family?

[*Note to reader*: Authorities have made confirmation of Mr. McKinley's existence, but have found no record of Mrs. Finch in that neighborhood, nor can they confirm her existence.]

October 10, 1993

I tried to talk to Jason this morning about how he feels. He told me he feels fine and has never felt better, but he had this strange look in his eyes like he hated me, and he said it with a devious smile that made me feel so uncomfortable I could not look him in his eyes. He just kept staring at me. His eyes were red like he had not slept in days. I asked him why he was spending so much time away from the family. He told me that he did not have a family anymore, and that he was an orphan looking for a new family! His words sent me into such a shock that I could not respond for a second. When I did speak the combination fear and shock made my voice crack, and that seemed to make him happy, but the look did not change. The smile just grew more sinister. I told him that we love him, and that he is all I have now that mom and dad are gone, and then I began to cry. I reached out to hug him and he grabbed my arms, looked at me, and said, "I guess you don't have anything, then!" I couldn't believe it! He just turned around and walked out.

I don't know what has happened to him. He used to be so kind and sweet. We got into fights like most siblings do, but the majority of the time we got along. I thought he was mom and dad's favorite but he always treated me like his kid sister. I don't understand what is happening. I am losing everything that I have. Why? The way he was looking at me sends chills up my spine. I am still shaking right now. It was like he wanted to kill me! I am so afraid of him right now. He is probably the one who killed mom and dad. I just can't understand why he would do something like that. I have got to find out why this happened and tell the cops. I know what I'm going to do. I am going to call that dude Erick and ask him if he wants to go to a movie or something.

6:20 p.m. I just got off the phone with Erick and he said that we could go out to the bowling alley. He said he is not much of a movie person, which is weird 'cause he asked me if he could take me to a movie before. I am almost scared to go out with him but I have to if I want to find out what is going on with Jason. I have to get ready—he will be here at 8:30!

October 11, 1993

It's midnight and I just got home. I'm freaked out! Eric was late and picked me up at 9:30 and took me to the bowling alley. When we got there he said he forgot his money at home.

We were standing at the cash register and I didn't have money for both of us, so I was stuck. Then he says, "We'll just swing by the house and go grab it—come on!" We drove up to the hills and when I asked him if he lived up here he just looked at me and smiled. He did not say a word. So I waited a second and asked him much longer until we got to his house. Again he smiled and said nothing. At that point I told him I wanted to go home because it was going to take too long to grab his money and get back to the bowling alley. This time he didn't look at me, he just drove faster. When I asked him to please slow down, he sped up. I started to cry because I thought he was going to kill me. Then he pulled off to a dirt path, which turned out to be a driveway to an old abandoned shed-type house. He turned around to look at me and asked me why I was crying. I said, "Because you are scaring me." Then he said, "How am I scaring you?" I looked at him like he was crazy and he was giving me back the same look, as if he honestly didn't know what he had done. So I said, "Who lives here?" He told me nobody lives here anymore, and that he keeps things here that are of value to him. I asked him, "Why would you have to hide your valuables?" He turned to me, laughing, and said, "So nobody will steal them, silly!" Then before I could ask him anything else he got out of the car.

I watched him walk toward the house but the fog was thick and it was dark. The place was covered with trees. You couldn't even see the sky, and what was worse was the wind was blowing hard in big gusts that seemed to rock the car back and forth. He was gone for more than fifteen minutes when a flashlight shined in the car through the front windshield, then another one shined through the driver's side window, then another one on the passenger's side window. I was so scared because I knew it had to be more than just Erick doing it. The car was filled with lights from all sides, and I couldn't see outside. I closed my eyes and started screaming. Then the driver's door opened, and I heard Erick's voice saying, "Sarah, what's wrong?" I looked at him and saw the flashlights were gone. Then I said, "Who were the people shining flashlights in the car?" He looked at me and said, "Sarah, there is nobody up here but me and you!" I said, "I want to go home!" He told me, "It must have been some type of reflection or something!" I was in such a hurry to just get out of there I didn't argue about what I had seen. I just wanted him to take me home.

When we were almost to my house, he said that if I want to meet Amon-Ra, all I have to do is ask. I said, "Excuse me?" Then he looked at me as if I was crazy, turned down the radio, and said, "Sarah, I did not say anything! Are you feeling all right?" I said, "No, I guess I'm just stressed out." When I looked up we were in front of my house—I didn't even feel the car stop I was so tripped out. I got out of the car and told him good-bye.

He just looked off. I was shaking so bad I couldn't put the key in the door and when I looked back at him he was just smiling at me in the car. When the door to my house finally unlocked and opened, I was so happy I didn't know what to do.

I can't stop shaking right now! This night was so strange. I have never been so afraid in my life. If I never see him again I'll be so happy. I didn't even find out anything about my brother other than his friend is crazy! I wonder who those people were shining those lights in the car? When we came in and when we left, I did not see any other cars around! I have to get some sleep and call Heather in the morning! I think they're coming to get me.

[**Note to reader**: *Authorities have never confirmed Erick's existence. Additionally, the location in the Hollywood hills referenced in Sarah's entry on October 11, 1993 matches the description of the spot where Sarah's parents' car was found.*]

October 12, 1993

Heather sounded really strange this morning when I asked her to come over—like someone was standing there listening to our conversation. She sounded so vague! When I tried to tell her about what happened with Erick, she just cut me off and said, "School sucks!" I was like, "Heather, what are you talking about? Are you all right?" She said, "Yeah, I'm fine, but I have to go right now and do my homework!" Then she just hung up on me. All day yesterday she was gone and when I finally reached her she doesn't wanna talk and sounds real weird. I hope everything is all right with her. I'm worried.

Jason just came back home after being gone for two days, and he really smells like he hasn't taken a shower in a long time. He came in my room and said, "Did you have fun with Erick?" He had that same drugged, hate-filled look in his eyes and that sinister smile on his face that says you're next. Then he just closed the door and walked off before I could reply. He looks so bad! I wish I could do something to save him, but he needs help and I can't give it to him. I'm going to talk to Uncle Harry about this again and see if we can get Jason some counseling or rehab 'cause he looks like he's on drugs. Once I tell Uncle Harry about the money I found in Jason's room and what happened the other night with Erick, he will understand and get Jason some help. It's time. Jason needs to go.

10:05 p.m. I spoke with my uncle about Jason, and he told me that it sounded serious. He is going to do something about Jason's spending so much time away from home. He also said that he was going to get some counseling for me and Jason. I was happy when I heard that, and then Jason came home just to grab something. I stopped him and told him Uncle Harry wanted to talk to him. He looked at me as if I wasn't even there, like he was looking through me or something. I heard Uncle

Harry's voice come from behind me and say, "Jason, we need to have a talk before you go anywhere." Jason said, "I have a date tonight. I have to go right now—she's waiting for me." He just walked past my uncle and said, "I'll talk to you later," and then he was gone. I have lost all hope of reaching Jason. It does not seem like anyone can reach him right now. I just hope that uncle Harry can talk to him tomorrow and get him some help. My poor brother! Heather called. She's coming over tomorrow. We are going to go to the library and research old news clippings of the Blue Man scandal. I want to know more about him. I think he is responsible for the change in my brother's behavior. I need to find some peace. First my parents. Now my brother.

CHAPTER 3
Heather and Sarah's Last Trip: The Investigation

October 14, 1993

Tonight, I'm going to steal my aunt's car, pick up Heather and go by Old Man McKinley's house to see what we can find out. Yesterday at the library we found out that Old Man McKinley went to trial over the gypsy robberies, but he was acquitted and the others were convicted. I think that Old Man McKinley is a gypsy and is brainwashing my brother, so I am going to get some answers. Jason came home yesterday and spoke with my uncle. I think everything must have gone well because Jason is still home. I'll find out more later but Jason is supposed to check into a rehab place. Well, I have to go. It's working.

October 15, 1993 – I Like Lindsey

We sat in front of Old Man McKinley's house all last night and nothing happened. My aunt didn't even notice that the car was driven all last night. That's good, because I'm definitely going to need to use it again. I am so tired right now, but I must write this down before I forget it. I had a deep conversation with Heather last night. I had no idea that she was as smart as she is. I always kind of took her for just a slow burnt-out girl, but she is very smart. She is very wise when it comes to people, their actions, and their basic profile. I never really ever thought about things or the world in that way before. I mean she really made me think about things that seemed so unimportant before, but now that my eyes have been opened, I realize those things are very important.

Heather talked to me about this girl in school who did not fit in and was awkward with the other kids in school. She would walk around through the halls sometimes singing songs under her breath very quietly. She was always at school -- every day, even before class started. It always seemed like she was the first to come and the last to leave. At the school dances she was always there but would never dance with anybody. She was quiet in class and never asked questions. When people tried to make friends with her, she would be unfriendly—not in a mean or nasty way; she would just be unresponsive and not talkative. In fact, she rarely talked at all. If you said, "Hello," she would say nothing. The kids at school called her Space Girl.

As time went on, the majority of the kids forgot all about her and basically ignored her altogether. New kids would notice her oddness, but soon, like with the others, she would become unimportant and unnoticed. Heather became intrigued by this odd girl and wanted desperately to become her friend. So one day Heather began to just sit by her and occasionally make eye contact and smile. Then she began to imitate some of the girl's actions, like putting a flower in her hair or drawing shapes on the ground with rocks. Heather said no matter how early she got to school, the girl was already there. So Heather decided to get to school when the gates opened up, and when she pulled up there was the girl standing in front of the school waiting for the gates to open. Heather walked up, looked at the girl and smiled, and the girl smiled back. Then the girl spoke and told Heather her name. It was Lindsey.

Lindsey began to talk to Heather. She told Heather how smart she was for watching her all this time and picking up her habits. During school they would have to pretend that they did not talk. After school sometimes they would meet in the woods so they could talk. Lindsey and Heather began to play this game called Profile. They would pick people out of the yearbook and watch their habits. They'd watch everything—the classes they took, when they got to school, when they left, who their friends were, how they dressed, the routes they took to class, what they ate for lunch, how they groomed themselves, and basically everything there was to notice about them.

Lindsey had been playing this game the whole time. She could tell you when a person was going to walk past. She knew when teachers were likely to give a surprise test. She was so good at this game that talking to people was irrelevant to her, because when you approached her she already knew you were coming and what you wanted. Lindsey opened Heather's mind to people—how simple they are, and how simply the majority of people think. Lindsey said, "Take her, for instance. People think she is weird and crazy because she doesn't talk to or socialize with them. They don't know a thing about her, but she knows everything about them. So who is stupid, her or them?" She told Heather that no matter what you think about a person, they all hold something of value in their head and it's up to you to get it out of their head and into yours. I asked Heather where Lindsay is 'cause we could sure use her help right now. Heather said that Lindsey just stopped going to school one day and was never seen again. Nobody even noticed she was gone. To them, she had been gone a long time ago. That's really sad because they don't even know how close to them she really was.

We talked about so much more, like the universe, where we come from, and what we are here for. It was a really interesting night for me and I feel I became closer with Heather. I still wish I could have found out something, anything, about Mr. McKinley, but what I learned tonight was of great value to me. I'm so burnt out right now. I have to get some sleep.

October 16, 1993 – He's Gone

Jason left this morning for a treatment place to get help for his drug addiction. My uncle told me that Jason was on cocaine. That didn't come as a shock to me. I never thought Jason would use cocaine but I'm not surprised he did. I'm just glad that he is getting some help away from here. Heather is supposed to come over tonight with some news. Hopefully we can find out more.

October 17, 1993

Heather said that Mrs. Finch wants her to feed the cat while she visits some friends. Mrs. Finch left Heather the key to the house and said she will be gone for one week. So I'm packing my things and I'm going to stay with Heather at Mrs. Finch's house. I told my aunt I'm staying at Heather's and left Mrs. Finch's number as Heather's. I'm so glad to have Heather as a friend. She got on home study and everything to help me with this project. I hope some of my concerns will be answered, because the new ones are making the old ones more troubling to me. I wonder who turned Jason on to cocaine. Well, I have to go and finish packing.

October 20, 1993

I have finally seen old man McKinley, and I now understand why they call him the blue man. His skin looks like fish or something — blue and silvery, shinier than normal skin, stretched tight over his body. It was late, about 11:00 last night, when I saw him. He wheeled himself outside, lit a cigarette, and just stared at the full moon. I would have missed him had Heather not just happened to glance out of the window. We had already been there for two days and Heather was teaching me how to play the Profile game. We were watching Old Man McKinley's house and he would not open up blinds or curtains during the day. At night, he would not turn on any lights until after 9:00 p.m. We had a debate on whether he was sleeping or not. I think he sleeps during the day and wakes up at night, but Heather said that she is not sure about that because Mrs. Finch told her that some days all of his blinds are open. She thinks his sleeping schedule depends on what he is doing.

We still have not seen anything out of the ordinary, like kids coming by or something, so I have to go back there again tonight. I really hope I find out something, but I really don't know what I expect to find. Maybe I'm just losing my mind and running in circles. My brother is getting help for his problems and it's not like this old man could have murdered my parents—he can't even walk. I can't use this. This information is going to be useless. I need to talk to Heather; I need better information. This isn't working.

The night before last, I had a dream that Heather, Erick, Alex, and Ericka were all standing over me while I was tied up in the bed. I could not speak or move—all I could do was look. Then

Ericka put a pillow over my face and it really felt like I couldn't breathe, then I woke up. I wonder what it meant? I am losing it. I think I'm going to talk to Heather about it. I'm scared to tell her about it, but I don't know why. Well, I have to go finish getting packed and have my aunt take a look at this spider bite on my arm. Mrs. Finch has so many spiders at her house, it is really creepy. Well, I have to hurry 'cause I'm taking the bus back to Mrs. Finch's house.

October 23, 1993 – Magic Trick

Two days ago, we finally saw something worth watching. Two young girls came by old man McKinley's house about 3:00 a.m. It wasn't like we had to sit and watch to see them -- they came by laughing and carrying on. I'm surprised they didn't wake up the whole neighborhood. They looked intoxicated or high on something. Heather grabbed the camera and began taking pictures of them. I hope we got good pictures so we can see their faces but I doubt it. They went into Old Man McKinley's with a key, or the door was unlocked because they just walked in. They were in there for an hour or two when a man walked out of the house, got into the girls' car, and drove off. We got pictures of him too. The girls' car was a newer green Jeep Cherokee. The lights went off at dawn, and Heather and I took shifts watching the house. I took the first shift until 1:00 p.m., and there was no movement inside the house as far as I could tell. The man had not come back with the car.

When I woke up around 8:00pm Heather was wide awake watching the house. At 11:00 p.m. the lights still had not come on. I found that very strange. I was about to give up at 2:00 a.m. when the Jeep pulled up, and the same two girls got out of the car laughing and carrying on, almost identical to the night before. They stayed inside for an hour, and again the man came out of the house and left in the Jeep. Heather and I were in shock. It was like watching a horror movie or something. I was so freaked out right then, I could not believe it. How did the girls leave the house? How did the man get back into the house? We were watching the house the whole time. It's impossible! I don't know what to do or think. It seems like everywhere I look for answers, I find more questions. This whole thing gets more complicated with every passing day. I'm starting to wonder if it's me!

Mrs. Finch comes home tomorrow, so I had to leave just in case she comes early or something. I helped clean up and stuff before I left. It's just, I'm so tired of all this. I feel like I'm so close to the truth about what really happened, but I'm just looking in the wrong direction. Heather dropped the film off and we should have it in a few days. I wish I could watch old man

54

McKinley's house just a little more. I have to find out how those girls were able to leave the house while we were watching and how the man got back in. Well, I have to help my aunt with some things and then do my homework. I'm running on fumes right now!

8:15 p.m. I'm freaked out right now. I still cannot believe what I just saw when I was out with my aunt. I am so terrified right now. When I saw him my skin just crawled. He looked at me with that same look Jason had in his eyes, and that sinister smile like "I'm going to get you." I couldn't believe they were together. Alex and Erick had been following me and my aunt from the post office to the supermarket. I noticed the Jeep instantly in the passenger side mirror. Everywhere we went that Jeep went with us. At first I had no idea who was in the car or why they were following us, but when we got to the supermarket they pulled up alongside of us, looked at me and laughed. Then they drove off! I was in so much fear and shock, all I could let out was a gasp. My aunt was so oblivious to the situation; she thought I was having an asthma attack or something. She was like, "Are you all right, honey?" I could barely get out the word yes. She offered me some water and I gladly took it. I started to tell her, but I decided against it because she might have thought I was crazy.

When I got back, I tried to call Heather but she didn't pick up the phone. I think I'm going to talk to my uncle about our security because I have reason to believe we are in danger, based on what happened with Jason and my parents. I can't begin to explain in detail why, 'cause he wouldn't understand.

I know now that something is really wrong. I saw Alex in the same car that did the magic trick in front of Old Man McKinley's, and he was with my brother's friend Erick. The worst part is, they were following us. They are watching me. I'm not watching them—they are watching me. What do they want? I am not going to let them get me before I get them.

October 24, 1993

I can't go back to sleep! It's three in the morning right now and the nightmares are too much. The noises in the house are keeping the horror going. I don't know what's worse, the nightmares or being awake! This time I had a dream that Old Man McKinley was in my house sealing the front door shut. All of the other doors and windows were already sealed. The house had this strange red glow to it that made his color seem normal. As he started to wheel towards me I turned to run, but I turned right into Alex's arms and he grabbed me. Then Erick came into the room with a knife saying, "If you don't shut up,

I'll shut you up forever!" As he got closer, his face turned into Jason's and I woke up.

I don't know what that could have meant, but my mind is out of control and I need help. The only problem is that I can't tell anyone about this. The only person who would understand is Heather, but every time I try to tell her, I start to feel awkward, like I can't approach her about all of my dreams. It's almost like I feel she could be one of them, but I know that is impossible. I just don't know what to do. Erick and Alex are friends, and I have to find out what is going on with them. I wonder if my brother ever met Alex? He would have to have met him. I hope that when he comes home from rehab I can talk to him about this. He holds the answers to so many of my questions. I just know it. I have to take my mind off this for awhile, 'cause this is driving me crazy. I've got to go.

October 25, 1993

I talked to my uncle yesterday about us being in danger, and to my surprise he was open-minded and very receptive to my feelings. I told him about Erick and the whole flashlight thing. I want Erick gone. I even told Uncle Harry about Old Man McKinley but he didn't show much concern about the Old Man, even though he remembered the story! I couldn't tell him how Heather and I were watching the Old Man from Mrs. Finch's house, but I did tell him about how Alex and Erick had been following me and Auntie Nancy. He thought we should go to the police. I told him I already went to the police when Ericka died, and I found a mug shot of Alex and the police told me he was dead. My uncle is going to check with some friends on the history of the man that was in the police mug shot book. My uncle's getting close. He doesn't think I'm crazy.

It feels good to have him so willing to help me. I was so afraid to talk to him about it. He told me how he wanted to have a memorial service for my mom and dad, but my grandparents don't want to believe my parents are dead. My grandparents are mad at my uncle because he had the missing persons case turned into a homicide case. I feel bad for my uncle. He is going through a lot. He told me that he wants to go to San Francisco on the 27th, and that it would be good for all of us to go. I'm looking forward to it. I keep trying to call Heather, but she has not been home. I hope she is all right. My uncle said by the time we get back, he should have some info on Alex. Well, I have to go do some more schoolwork. Will write more later.

November 4, 1993 – Back from the trip

I know now that they are going to kill me or my family! They must be watching my every move. I tried to call Heather when I came home last night and she is still not home. I hope she is all right! They probably knew we were watching from Mrs. Finch's house. God, I hope nothing happened to Heather after I left her at Mrs. Finch's house. It's all my fault! I'm scared right now! Everything was so perfect and relaxing for the first two days. Then while we were at Pier 39, I wandered off from my aunt and uncle to look at the bay. I was thinking how peaceful it was watching the birds and the waves. My aunt knew where I was because she could still see me. I didn't want to be bothered with the tourist shops and all the noisy people. I wanted to enjoy the scenery of San Francisco—not the people. I was in my own little world when this girl tapped me on my shoulder. I was startled by her touch. She asked me if I knew how to get to Haight Street? As I looked at her face, it seemed so familiar but I could not place it. I told her I was not from around here and that I'm on vacation. She looked at me with that sinister smile and said thank-you with a chuckle. At that moment I knew exactly how I knew her. She was dressed differently, but it was Candy from Alex's house, who said she was Erick's sister when I saw her again. My heart was racing a million miles an hour as I watched her walk off. I wanted to tell my uncle, but I was frozen with fear. By the time I got hold of my thoughts, she had disappeared into the moving crowd.

My aunt came out of one of the shops with some bags and was asking me to look at some of the stuff she had gotten. I could barely focus on the things she was showing me. I wanted to tell her right then but I would have sounded crazy, and I can't say I wasn't at the time. As always, she was so oblivious to my panic and fear. She just continued showing me the things she found. Her attitude threw off my thoughts. I even thought to myself that it must be my mind overreacting to all the trauma I've been through lately. I went into the shop with my aunt and tried to block it out!

Everything was going great. We had such a fun time after that! We toured Alcatraz, climbed Coit Tower, drove across the Golden Gate Bridge, and went to the movies! We were having a great time and I was enjoying myself so much I had almost totally forgotten about Candy. Then one night, in the lounge area at the hotel I was reading a magazine waiting for my aunt and uncle to come down for our dinner reservation. I wasn't even paying much attention to the person next to me until she spoke and said, "Why haven't you been to the Haight district yet?" I looked over and it was Peaches from Alex's house. My breath left my body like someone had just jumped from behind me and said, "Boo!" She stood up and said, "You should really go and check it out!" Then she walked out the front door.

I started to cry. They won't stop playing this sick game with me and my family and I don't know why. When my uncle and aunt came down from our suite, I had drawn a small crowd of concerned people. I was a mess of tears! I don't really remember anything else after that, 'cause I passed out! When I woke up, I was in the hotel suite, and a physician was taking my pulse. I asked what happened. He said over-excitement to my system because of extreme shock caused me to faint. My uncle and I talked for a real long time and he thinks I should get some help for this. Uncle Harry even cried because he blames himself for not being there for me. He said he should have been more comforting to me and Jason. I felt so sorry for him. I told him that it's not his fault. There are people who are trying to hurt us. That seemed to make him cry harder. I don't think he believes what I'm trying to tell him. I can't tell him any more about what is going on—it's too upsetting to him. I love my uncle a lot, and I don't want to cause him any more pain. He needs to be free from this misery.

Today, I am going to help my aunt with her garden. After our vacation, I promised myself I would do more to bond with my aunt and uncle. They are all I have left in this world. I do have other relatives but I don't know them. Aunt Nancy and Uncle Harry are the closest thing to parents I have. I have to go!

November 5, 1993

I still have not spoken with Heather, and I'm really starting to worry. I wish I could go to her house. She always told me not to go to her house because her parents are really strict, which does not make a lot of sense to me, considering how much she stays out. They even let her take home study when she asked for it. I'm really worried about her, and I can't do anything but wait. I just hope everything is all right with her!

November 6, 1993

My uncle showed me a picture of Alex today and he asked me, "Is this the man who was friends with Ericka?" I told him, "Yes!" My uncle asked me to sit down and he had a worried look on his face. I asked him, "What's wrong?" He told me that Alex is not the man's name, and that he was picked up on a domestic disturbance after he stole his wife's car one night. That's the only reason his picture was even in the mug shot book. He was involved in a horrible car accident that killed his wife and child. No one survived! I told my uncle I know that's him and my uncle told me, "He was identified by his dental records. He died in the car accident." My uncle told me that I must be mistaken about the person I have seen, and the similarities in the two men may be so striking that I can't tell the difference. I told my uncle that "It may be possible that I may have the two men confused, but that man looks so much like the guy Ericka used to go out with that we should use that picture as a description." My uncle told me he already did that! It is such a relief to have my uncle helping me with this. I told him where Alex used to live and to send the police over there. If we can figure out what happened to Ericka and her family, we may find some answers as to what happened to my parents. He told me that he would give the detective on the case the information on where the guy lived. I really hope that we can find out some answers about Alex, 'cause he is the mastermind of all this—I just know it.

November 7, 1993 – The Prodigal Son

My uncle read a letter from Jason to us last night! He said that Jason can write a letter to us, but cannot receive mail for another month. I really wanted to write to him. I miss him. He sounds like he is doing so well and like he's getting better. Bastard. He said he misses us, loves us all very much, and that he hates the food! My uncle said that Jason will be home in January because he is doing really well in the program. That made me really, really, really happy to know my brother will be home soon. I can't wait to see him again. Well, I better get on this schoolwork. My job is never done.

November 9, 1993 – My Only Friend

Yesterday, Heather just showed up at my house with her bags, crying. I was so shocked by her appearance that I couldn't say anything at first. We went up to my room, and before I could close the door she was pulling out a bottle of alcohol from her bag. She sat down on the bed and was mumbling to herself while drinking like one of those street people. I got control of my thoughts enough to ask her, "What's wrong?" She told me that her dad had slapped her and tried to punch her in the stomach. Then she lifted her shirt to show me knuckle-mark bruises, as if to emphasize her point. My mouth was wide open in shock, but before I could ask her why, she blurted out, "The bastard tried to kill my baby!"

At that point I was dumbfounded. I said, "Who is the father?" She looked at me with tears in her eyes and said, "Just some guy at school." I could not believe what I was hearing. Hell, I still can't believe it. She never talked about sex or her boyfriend. I asked her what she was going to do. She told me that she was not sure what she should do because she does not want to get an abortion, but she's too young to keep it. At that point, I noticed she was drinking, and that she couldn't do that if she expected to have a healthy baby. Before I could say something, she responded again about how she has to stop getting drunk and high. I told her that I would help her and I snatched the bottle out of her hand. She looked at me with such anger I thought she was going to hit me. Then her angry eyes turned soft as a puppy and she began to cry. She told me, "Thank you."

We had a good time talking last night about so many different things like boys and what we want to do with our lives. Heather told me she wants to be a social worker and help kids who are in messed up homes. I told her about my dream of becoming a D.A., so I can put criminals behind bars. When I asked her if she wanted to stay with us until the baby was born, she said, "Yes!" I told her all I have to do is talk with my uncle about it in the morning. I told her he would say yes, but he would probably want to speak with her parents about it. She got this terrified look on her face and said, "No, he can't call my parents!" She was so scared she was shaking. I told her I would see if he could do it without calling but I couldn't promise anything. She told me if he had to call, then she would just stay somewhere else.

When I woke up this morning, she was gone but she left a note that said she was going to her cousin's house up north, and that she would send word back when the baby was born. I cried a lot this morning and I'm still kind of hurt. I wish I could help her. I'm really going to miss her a lot; she's my only friend. I wish she would have left a telephone number for me to call. She'll probably call when she gets up there and give me the number. I still have not told her what happened while I was in San Francisco.

I guess since I don't have Heather, it's up to me. I don't care if it's just me, I'm going to finish this. She left with the pictures we took at Old Man McKinley's. What am I going to do? I wonder if the detectives will get some information from that address. I miss you Heather.

November 11, 1993

My uncle told me that the detectives went to Alex's old address and spoke with his neighbors about him. Everyone they spoke with said they did not remember his face in the picture. The landlord said that the place was leased to a woman named Esperanza. It does not make any sense that the neighbors don't remember him. I spoke with one of the neighbors after Ericka's family was murdered, and he said he did not see them move. He obviously knew who I was talking about, but my uncle said, "They took his mug shot to all the residents in the building, and no one remembers him!" I wanted so badly to prove to my uncle that I wasn't crazy and that I really was with that guy Alex, but it was pointless. Everything points to me being crazy! I have nothing to back my words with, and all the proof is against what I have seen and know to be the truth.

My uncle has made an appointment for me to see a therapist tomorrow morning. I told him I know he thinks I'm crazy, but one day I will prove to him that I really am telling the truth. We are all in danger. He hugged me and told me he believes me and he knows I'm not crazy. It's just that he feels a therapist can help me deal with the loss of Mom and Dad. At that point, I started crying! Maybe I was crying because of my frustration. Maybe I was crying because I had not thought of Mom and Dad in a few days, or maybe a little bit of both. One thing is for sure—I had a good long cry, and now I am completely emotionally drained.

November 12, 1993

I just came back from the therapist and I never knew how much pain truly ran through my body. She told me to tell her what's happened in my life since coming to California, the flashbacks alone brought tears to my eyes. It was very emotional! I have had so much loss in my life in such a brief period of time. She asked me to describe my feelings about Ericka's death, my parents' disappearance, my brother, and Heather. We decided to break down each individually, which took up all the time. I did not get a chance to finish. I was talking about my parents when our time was up.

She suggested that I try to just enjoy being a teenager for one week, and do normal teenage activities like movies, malls, and being around other teenagers if possible. I told her I don't know any other teenagers and I'm scared to go outside to places by myself. She told me we will talk about it further when we meet again next week.

I like my therapist! She seems like a really nice person. Her name is Dr. Linda Jones and she has lived in L.A. for a short time like me. The only thing I don't like about the therapy is the time. An hour is too short! When we really started to talk about things, it was time to go. Dr. Jones told me that the first visits are like that, but as time moves on, we are going to get to the root of the problem. I really hope so, because I don't want to be screwed up like this anymore.

CHAPTER 4
Jackie & Owen

November 13, 1993

This morning I told my aunt what Dr. Jones had suggested, and asked her if she would like to go to the mall with me this afternoon. As usual my Aunt Nancy, always ready to shop and spend my uncle's money, was like, "Anything for you, princess!" It felt really good to be out just enjoying myself and doing normal things. My aunt is like a teenager herself. We went to all the cool stores like Eddie Bauer, Gap, and J. Crew. When we got to the last store, I was so tired and worn out. My aunt was trying on some clothes in the dressing room when this girl came up to me and asked me where I got my jacket. At first, I was not in the mood to meet anyone new, and then I thought about what Dr. Jones said, "Be a teenager. Be around other teenagers."

I told her I got the jacket in Arizona, and she was like, "What part of Arizona were you in?" I told her, "I'm from Phoenix!" She was like, "I'm from Mesa!" That was it! We were talking nonstop for almost half an hour. Then my aunt came over and said she was ready to go. She'd obviously had enough of waiting for me. I started to leave, then I thought, "This girl is really cool. We should hang out." I asked her for her number. She gave it to me and I gave her mine. We're supposed to go hang out tomorrow afternoon at the mall again, catch a movie or something. I had a good day today and I can't wait to tell Dr. Jones about Jackie from Pasadena. Well, I have to put my clothes away!

November 14, 1993

Jackie is so cool! We hung out at the mall by ourselves for a while until we ran into some of her friends—this guy named Owen (who is so cute!), Paul and Steven. We went over to Paul's house and had so much fun. The guys had some pot and I was scared to smoke in front of Jackie 'cause I wasn't sure if she smoked. She really didn't look like the type, but when Steven passed her the bong, she took the fattest rip out of all of us and didn't choke. I was so shocked!

We were listening to Led Zeppelin, Janis Joplin, and the Doors. I was totally vibing to the whole thing and kept thinking how natural it all felt. No worries, no fears, just being a teenager. Then Owen came over and started talking to me, which at first was embarrassing, because I was way too high. I could barely form a sentence and I had a grin on my face that would not go away like the Joker from Batman or something. I can't even recall much of what he was saying because my mind was on so many other things. All I know is, he is so cute and he is 19. Luckily Jackie noticed my situation and came to save me, which was so cool. She came over and said, "Your mom is picking you up at my house in 20 minutes. We've got to go!" I got up and told Owen that it was nice to meet him and I'll see him later. I was so high it came out so uncool. I don't think he cared much.

Steven drove us to Jackie's house and he was totally trying to get Jackie to go out with him. She was not really into him and I think that was clear to all of us. Once we got inside, her mom was the only one home, and Jackie introduced us. I was like, "You have a lovely home, Mrs. Keller." She looked at me, smiled, and said, "Thank you." Then we went up to Jackie's room. I was like, "Your mom knows I'm high, Jackie!" She was like, "Don't even trip. My mom doesn't care about stuff like that." I thought that was so cool! Then her mom knocked on the door and asked were we hungry 'cause she's ordering some pizza. That was so right on time! Mrs. Keller told me to call my house and see if it's all right if I eat dinner there tonight. I was like, "All right!" Mrs. Keller talked to my aunt and they totally hit it off. Jackie's mom is so cool! I wish my Mom had been like that.

Jackie and I ate pizza and talked about things we like to do when we are high. She told me she likes to go outside and look up at the stars, feel the wind blowing, and imagine the world spinning. She does not look like the type! She is one of those girls who look like they are stuck up and full of themselves—blond hair, blue eyes, and everything she has is designer. I was totally not expecting her to have a mom like that or smoke pot. She doesn't drink, but I think I can change that. I told her about Owen and she was like, "That's so cool!" She told me she is going to hook up a double date with us.

November 16, 1993

Jackie called me this evening and told me that we are on for Saturday. She said we might not go to the movies, but we are going miniature golfing. I have never been miniature golfing before. I don't even know what to wear. I'm going to have to call her back and ask her. Oh my God, look how I sound! I don't even know anything about this guy. He could have a girlfriend for all I know. He may not even like me and is just going out with us because Steven asked him. See, I'm making too much out of this. I have to go!

November 19, 1993

Dr. Jones had me do some exercises, which still have me a little shaken up. She asked me to act as if my parents were in front of me, and talk to them as if they were leaving forever. It was very emotional for me but it felt good to say what I had been keeping inside. Dr. Jones said that she was troubled by the fact that I blamed myself for what happened to my parents. She said next time I come for therapy we are going to go a little deeper into that. We also talked about my date tomorrow and how I felt about going out with a boy after so long. My doctor asked me, "What do I want to gain out of the situation?" That really had me stuck. I am not sure what I want or expect to gain from this. Her question did open my eyes to the reasons I'm feeling the way I am. I think I should just go out to have a good time, and if something comes out of it, then I'll deal with that when it comes. I really do enjoy my time with Dr. Jones. It helps me out a great deal. In just two visits I am already feeling so much better. Well, I have to go!

November 21, 1993

        I had so much fun last night! Owen is different than I expected. He is into hip-hop music and reggae. My first impression of him was that he was a stoner. I was so off! Heather would be disappointed in me, because I failed the Profile game. Well, I was baked out of my mind, so how could I have profiled him accurately?

        Owen was so cool with his baggy jeans and his baseball hat covering his eyes. I took his hat off to look at those eyes, and we started wrestling for his hat. He felt so good, like he works out or something. I was so tempted to kiss him, but I thought about my talk with Dr. Jones, and I held back, which was so hard 'cause Owen is so cute. He is so funny. He did an impersonation of the fat guy who gave us our equipment and almost had me in tears. He had the guy's voice and walk down perfectly. Maybe it was because I was high, but he had me laughing all night.

After we left the miniature golf place we went in Owen's car to the Hollywood hills to look at the view and smoke. His car is nice! It's one of those classic cars, and it is so fast and powerful. He has a really nice sound system too. You can hear the car for miles. We got out and talked for a while about what it would be like to go into outer space. I was so into his every word. I was having so much fun, but I had to go home. I made a pact with my aunt that I'd be home by midnight. Not like she'd notice anyway. Owen understood and was the perfect gentleman. He asked me for my number and told me he would like to hang out sometime!

I went to sleep last night and all I could think about was him. He is so cool! I had to call Jackie and thank her for last night. She was like, "It's no big deal," and she had a good time with Steven. Surprise! Jackie & I are supposed to go out shopping after Thanksgiving on Friday.

November 25, 1993

Owen just called to wish me Happy Thanksgiving and invite me to a party he and his friends are throwing on Saturday. We talked for an hour! I'm so excited right now. I have to call Jackie and tell her about this. I hope she comes!

November 28, 1993

I had so much fun with Owen last night at the party. Jackie came too, and she got drunk! She only had some beer, but she couldn't handle it. I had never been to a party like that before. They had a DJ and three kegs! Owen and his friends made money by selling cups for five dollars each. Some other dudes tried to use their own cups; Owen's friends surrounded the dudes and took their cups. Owen is the ringleader of his friends. He was dictating what was happening. He told the guys who brought their own cups that if they wanted to drink from the kegs to buy a cup and if they were caught sharing the same cup there was going to be trouble. Most of Owen's friends were big like football players, and it turned out most of them were.

Owen was selling weed there, too. Well, not just him—he had his friends selling for him. It seemed like every 10 minutes someone was giving him some money. It felt good to be his date. The other girls looked at me like they hated me, but I didn't mind that at all. Owen kept introducing me to so many people I couldn't possibly remember their names. He was the coolest guy at the party, and he knew it. I was so attracted to his confidence and power that I just could not help but give him a kiss. We took a ride around the hills and talked about how happy he was no fights had broken out at the party. He told me that usually a fight would have broken out by then. I was so entranced by him that I was speechless. I mean everything he did was just so amazingly cool. I was totally into his every word.

While he was talking, his cell phone rang, and he was like, "I have to swing by this house real fast." He asked me to reach under my seat and hand him the bag. I felt the bag, and it was a plastic bag full of weed. He put the bag inside his leather coat, zipped it up, and got out of the car. He was gone for about five minutes, and when he came out he gave me a whole bunch of loose money. He told me to organize it into hundred dollar stacks, which I had no idea how to do. Then he showed me! Every time I count a hundred, fold it in half, and lay it the opposite way as the first hundred stack. When I was done I had counted $2,100 dollars even. He told me, "Good—that's how much I thought would be there!" He dropped me off and told me he would call me tomorrow. He also gave me some weed to smoke! When I woke up this morning, it all felt like a dream. I had to call Jackie and ask her why she didn't tell me how cool Owen was.

She told me that it did not seem important, 'cause I already liked him, which makes sense, I guess.

Now I don't know what to do about telling Dr. Jones about him, 'cause he sells drugs and stuff. I'm supposed to be honest about my feelings and what's going on in my life if I expect to get help with my problems. I guess I'm going to have to tell her. A whole lot has happened in the week we missed because of Thanksgiving. Owen still has not called!

November 30, 1993

I spoke with my uncle about going to school. He said that he would have to see if my going back to school is a good idea. I really want to go to regular school with the other kids my age. I want to be normal again! Jackie asked me why I didn't go to school. I told her because my parents want me to adjust to living in California! Jackie doesn't understand that, but I had to tell her something. She doesn't know about my parents. It makes me uncomfortable to talk about my family, and I don't want to explain my situation to anyone right now. I need to talk to Dr. Jones about this.

[*Note to reader*: *There is no record of Sarah meeting with any doctors during this period of her life. Sarah's medical records reflect no visits other than her regular checkups.*]

December 4, 1993

I just woke up from a dream about my parents. At first everything felt normal. My parents and I were in the living room of our old house in Arizona, and then that dude Alex appeared in the doorway with a knife.

I think my talk with Dr. Jones yesterday opened up a lot of wounds that I thought had healed. We picked up right where we left off two weeks ago, about why I blame myself for my parents' disappearance. I told Dr. Jones, "I feel as if my relationship with Ericka led her family's murderers to my parents." Dr. Jones asked me, "Why do you feel as if the same people who murdered Ericka's family are responsible for your parents' disappearance?" I told her all about the strange things that happened with Alex, the girls, and Erick. That took up mostly all of my time. Dr. Jones told me to forgive myself and understand that I did not have control over the situation, which I have to say is not true! She doesn't understand.

The memories of Alex, Erick, Old Man McKinley and the girls really brought back a lot of pain and fear. All yesterday I was struck by the same fear and anxiety I had when my parents first disappeared. Owen called me to see if I wanted to hang out over at his friends' house. I told him I was busy with some family stuff. He totally picked up my vibe and asked me if I was all right. I told him yes, everything is fine. He told me if I need somebody to talk to or just want to hang out give him a call. I thought that was nice, and as a matter of fact I'm going to call him to see if I can take him up on that offer. I need it! I'm back outside Heather. I miss you.

December 5, 1993

Owen is an amazing person. I called him yesterday to take him up on his offer, and I must admit that I called pretty early in the morning. In fact, I woke him up, but he told me he did not mind. I told him I would like to just go out today and get away from everything. He told me that I can't do that on an empty stomach, and said we should have breakfast first. I was like, "Cool." When he showed up at my house, he had some flowers and a teddy bear. I thought that was cute! He told me that he would like to meet my parents before we leave. My uncle was the only one home, 'cause my aunt was at the gym. Owen and my uncle hit it off great. Owen complemented my uncle's home and told my aunt that he was going to take me to breakfast and a movie. I could tell that my uncle really liked him!

For breakfast I was expecting some Denny's or something like that, but Owen took me to a nice mom-and-pop '50s-style diner in Hollywood. He wanted to know how I liked California in comparison to Arizona. He asked me what it was like in

Arizona. I really enjoyed talking to him. It was almost like a session with Dr. Jones.

After breakfast, we went over to Owen's place and I was shocked to find out he doesn't live with his parents. I can't say I was disappointed, but I was very shocked. Before I could ask him how long he has been on his own, he pulled out a huge bag of pot along with a scale and some sandwich bags. He told me that he must apologize, but he had to have this ready for tonight. I was like, "What's going on tonight?" He looked at me, smiled, and said, "Just my daily routine!" Then he went back to what he was doing and said, "Roll some up and fix yourself something to drink if you want! The liquor is in the cabinet." I went and fixed up some drinks and rolled up a joint. For the next hour, we bagged up the pot while smoking and drinking. It was very relaxing and quite fun, I must say.

Owen told me about how his father's been in prison for murder since he was a kid and how bad things were for him and his mother. I felt sorry for him. He was a man long before his time and his childhood ended tragically. If he was in pain or hurting, you couldn't tell by looking at him. He was a mask of calm and coolness. It made me even more attracted to him. When he told me his mom died of a drug overdose when he was 15. He and his brother had been on their own ever since. I was in tears. I was like, "Where did you guys live?" He told me that his brother was 22 when his mom died and they just stayed at the house until last year, when his brother went to jail for drug possession. He told me his brother will be home in another year, and then he will be able to stop working and go to school. He told me that his family is all in a motorcycle club, and that he is the black sheep of the family 'cause he doesn't want to ride. He said he just feels that the family has got to change and he is going to be the one to do it. I asked him if he still visits his dad and he told me, "Yes!" He said it's a really long trip to the prison, but on Christmas and his pop's birthday he always makes it. I thought that was sweet and sad at the same time.

I understand Owen so much better after yesterday! It all makes sense now! He is not at all the way I thought he was. He sells to survive because that's all he knows. It's like he said to me, "What kind of job is going to pay a 19-year-old enough money to support himself?" I understand his pain so well, but I just did not feel right telling him about what happened to my parents. I don't want to scare him off with all of that. I must admit that it sounds a little crazy. I feel closer to him than I've ever felt to anyone in my life. I think I'm in love with him. He is meeting me at the library tomorrow. I don't want my uncle to meet Owen because he might ask questions and not approve of me seeing him. So, I told my uncle I need to go to the library to research for a paper. Then I'm going to Jackie's house. I've got to call Jackie and clear everything up. Plus I have to tell her about Owen and me.

[**Note to reader**: *This period marks Sarah's only documented feelings on romantic love interests. Her feelings seem genuine, though no confirmation has been made regarding Owen's existence. Some believe "Owen" is a fictitious name created to protect his true identity.*]

December 9, 1993

My uncle said it was cool for me to go to high school next semester. My aunt took me to enroll today and the school looks cool. It's a lot nicer than the other high schools I've seen. I'm just glad that Jackie is going to be there with me. I told her yesterday that I was going to go to school with her. Owen dropped me off at her house and sold her some pot. She was so excited and was totally planning our time at school together. I love Jackie—she is so crazy! Well, I have to go Christmas shopping with my aunt right now. I'm happy!

December 10, 1993

My session with Dr. Jones was very relaxing today. We did not talk about my parents or Ericka at all. She wanted to know what was going on in my life. I told her about Owen and Jackie. I did not tell her that Owen sells pot or that he has his own place, but I did tell her about his family. I told her that I wanted to share my experiences with family tragedy with Owen,

82

but I just could not bring myself to do it. Dr. Jones told me that when the time is right and I am ready, only I can decide. If I force the issue, I may possibly regret my decision. That made me feel very good to know that I had not done anything wrong, and that when I am ready is when it will be right. Dr. Jones always makes me feel so much better. I told her about my decision to go to school and how excited I was about it. She told me as long as I feel comfortable about going back to school she can see nothing wrong about my decision. Then she asked me how I felt about coming every other week instead of every week. I told her that I saw nothing wrong with it, but in my mind I was thinking, why? As if she knew what I was thinking, she told me that my progress was excellent, and that weekly sessions are not necessary and we will go to bi-weekly, unless I feel otherwise. I understood that totally! She is slowly easing me back into the normalness of being human.

I have to get ready to go over to Jackie's house, 'cause Owen is coming to get us for one of his parties. I'm supposed to stay at Jackie's tonight, but I want to stay with Owen! Got to go!

December 11, 1993

I have never seen anything like that in my life. I was scared last night. Everything was so perfect and going so well. Then this guy starts pissing on the floor in Owen's friend's house, and that was it! Owen looked at the guy pissing, who was standing in a group of cheering friends, and said, "Dude, have you lost your freaking mind?" The guy looked at Owen and just laughed. Owen's friends rushed over there and started fighting with the cheering guys. It really scared me because I had never seen so many people fighting at once. Owen was in the heart of the action. I was so afraid for him! More of Owen's friends came and then Owen had the upper hand. They held one guy while Owen broke a phone over his head, and they threw another guy through a closed door. Those guys, once laughing and cheering, ran out of there with Owen's younger friends in chase. Then Owen gave me his keys and told me to go with Jackie back to his house.

I waited with Jackie at Owen's house for a long time. Then Owen came home and his lip was busted. I ran over to him and hugged him so tight. I told him I was so worried about him. He kissed me on my lips and said, "Baby, I'm all right! You should worry about the other guys." Then he started laughing. I was just so happy he was safe with me, 'cause that fight really scared me. He and Steven were counting the money they made from last night, while smoking and drinking; it was as if they'd just left an amusement park. They were cracking jokes about how they beat up the guys and reminiscing on other fights they had gotten into. It seemed to all just be a game to them. I tried to pretend it was no big deal, but some of the things they had been through sounded scary. Jackie asked Steven if she could take his car to get some food, and of course he said, "Yes!" Owen gave me $100 and said he would take care of everyone. We took the orders for the boys and left. As soon as we got outside, Jackie said, "You looked so uncomfortable in there! We need to talk, Sarah!" We got into Steven's convertible Mustang, Jackie said, "You don't really know anything about Owen, do you?" I was like, "No! What am I supposed to know about a guy I just started dating? My friends should tell me what I need to know!" She looked at me as if to say sorry because she could tell what she said had upset me. Then she said, "I know I should have told you more about him, but Owen is not the type of guy who likes people talking about his business. The stuff I have to tell you is personal." She looked at me like a mother telling her child not to draw on the walls, her finger pointing at me, "Don't repeat this to anyone!" I was like, "You have my word!" At that moment, I was a little scared to hear what she had to say, and I hesitated in my response to her. She was like, "See, that's why I didn't tell you anything. You're going to get me killed or something worse." Then she turned up the radio and was visibly upset. We rode in silence for quite some time.

When we got to the drive-through, she turned the radio down and we placed our orders. She turned the radio back up, but I turned it down again and told her how sorry I was. She said, "It just upsets me that you feel I'm not telling you something just to keep a secret." She dropped her head and sighed while staring at the money in her hand. She turned to me and said, "I'll tell you this much, OK! Owen is not what he appears to be, and pot is not the only things he sells. His brother is real bad news!" Then she pulled up to the window, paid for the food, and turned the radio up. I wanted to know more, but at the same time I didn't.

The fight had scared me bad enough. I don't want to hear any bad things about Owen, because I don't have anything else to love. When we got back to the house Jackie instructed me to "Act normal, as if nothing has been said!" When we got in the house, Owen and Steven were in the back room. I went to knock on the door to the room they were in and Jackie told me, "Don't!" Right then Owen came out of the room. He just looked different to me after that day. He barely touched any of his food and neither did Steven. The whole night was so weird, 'cause Owen and Steven were hyper. They went out and did not come back until dawn. I was in his bed waiting for him when he came back, and Jackie was in the other bedroom sleeping. When Owen came home, he was with some people, and he did not come into the bedroom. My curiosity got the best of me, and I went into the living room. My eyes were not ready for the sight I was seeing. There were two big scruffy-looking biker guys weighing what looked like pure crystal meth. When they saw me, they looked at me with what seemed to be shock for just a brief moment. Then one of them said, "Owen, you didn't say anything about us having some fun! I would have brought some condoms." My eyes opened with shock at what he had said. Then Steven said, "Man, we should have taken them home last night, dude!" Owen walked over to me and quietly told me to get ready 'cause Steven is going to take us home. I woke up Jackie and got ready. When I was done, Owen was gone, which I thought was rude because he didn't even say good-bye. Steven came back alone and asked us if we were ready. I asked him where was Owen and he looked at me and said, "Hurry up because I have something I have to do!"

When we went out to the parking lot I was expecting to get into his Mustang, but we got into a newer-model truck. We rode in silence until we got to Jackie's house. As I was getting out of the car, Steven said, "Owen is going to call you—he said sorry about tonight!" I told him thanks, but he didn't reply.

Once inside of Jackie's room, I was on her about what is going on with them 'cause that was weird. She told me, "Just don't get too involved with him because he is dangerous!" I asked her, "How?" She said, "I'm not going to tell you anything else!" Then she went downstairs and came back with her mom. They took me home!

I feel so weird right now, like I'm doing something wrong, or that I'm stupid or something. Why is it that every time I feel as if I am finally normal, everything becomes so strange? I really thought that Owen was just a normal, everyday person when I met him. Jackie is treating me like I'm just a stupid little kid or something; she doesn't know me very well. Why is my life going so badly all of a sudden, after one night? It seems like Owen is a completely different person or something. When I came home and got into my room, I couldn't hold back my tears. Now I can't stop crying because I feel crazy again. Why is this happening to me? How many people have a friend who is murdered along with her whole family, a brother who lost his mind using drugs, a mother and father who disappeared off the face of the earth—all in less than half a year? Then when I try to lead a normal life, this happens. I thought love was real. I don't know who Owen is.

December 16, 1993

Jackie just called me and asked me if I would like to come over tomorrow after school to hang out. I told her yes, but I felt like I should have said no. Where does she get off calling me out of the blue like nothing ever happened? What kind of friend neglects to tell you important things she knows about the guy you're dating? I don't care what Owen is going to do! She could have at least told me what I was getting into when I told her I liked him. The only reason I'm going over there tomorrow is to give her a piece of my mind about what she did!

6:30 p.m. Owen just called me... Why am I so weak for him? I wanted to tell him how rudely he treated me and that I never wanted to talk to him again, but when I heard his voice, my heart skipped a beat! All my thoughts were blank. He told me, sorry about what had happened, and said that he wanted to make it up to me with dinner on Saturday. Before I could tell him no, he told me how badly he had missed me and that he was happy I had not hung up on him. Again, my heart skipped a beat and my mind went blank. Then he told me that he wanted to explain his situation to me over dinner, so please don't deny him the opportunity. I told him OK!

I feel so stupid and weak right now because everything I wanted to say was not said. Just the mere sound of his voice was enough to put butterflies in my stomach. I was speechless! I was putty in his hands to be molded into whatever he wanted. I can't believe this, because I am usually a strong-minded person. I'm going down a dangerous road.

December 17, 1993

I just came back from Jackie's house, and I guess I have to forgive her, because she was scared. Now I'm just a little worried about what Owen has to tell me tomorrow night. Jackie said she doesn't know much about Owen, but she has heard a lot about his brother Jimmy. He is a murderer! I can't begin to explain how fearful that made me of Owen. She told me that no one knows for sure if Jimmy killed the guy, but one thing is for sure: people who have problems with their family end up hurt, or worse. She also told me that Owen is doing his brother's job while he is in prison. When I asked her what that was, she told me that he runs the crystal trade in these parts and anyone who tries to cut in on the action gets hurt. That's what happened to the last guy who crossed Jimmy. They found his body in the Hollywood hills.

After hearing all of that, I can understand her fear, because I am afraid of Owen myself right now. I just hope that tomorrow I can act normal around him and not be uncomfortable. The strange thing is, I still love him, in spite of what I heard!

December 19, 1993

Last night I had sex with Owen! I didn't want to put out so soon, but he just has this power over me where I can't say no.

90

Maybe it was just the way the night went? He is so mysterious, but at the same time, he seems vulnerable. He has such a way with words that makes you listen and not interrupt him. It's almost like listening to someone reciting poetry. He was gentle with me and so compassionate while making love. I didn't have to direct him where to kiss me on my body—he just knew exactly where to go. It got to the point where I wanted him inside me so badly, it was like waiting for Christmas to come the night before. I couldn't wait to open my presents. It was everything that I expected and a whole lot more. When we finished, my body was lifeless with exhaustion, dripping hot sweat from every pore. Owen left the room and came back with a cold glass of grape juice. He lay next to me and softly blew his cool breath all over my body. It felt so good! It was wonderful!

After that, we laid there spent. He told me he would like to explain some things so I can understand him better. He said that he wanted to be with me, but he did not want me to get into something that I didn't feel comfortable with. I told him that I was comfortable with what I've seen so far, and that anything more should not be that hard to deal with, 'cause I've been through a lot. He stared at me with warm, soft eyes and said, "The last thing I want is to lose you because my life is so complicated." After that he told me about his family. He saw his dad kill a man right in front of him and his older brother. He told me that he is over his brother's old job of moving crystal, and that the money he gets off selling weed is not what he lives off. He said that being with him could be dangerous at times and that I would have to always be alert and aware of my surroundings, because things could change drastically in a heartbeat. I asked him what he meant by things could change drastically? Then he told me a story of how he went on a drop with his brother, and a guy pulled a gun on the dude they were meeting and robbed all of them. He said things like that and worse can happen at any time. Then he laughed and said, "We got all our stuff back!" I asked him how? He told me that his brother is a real smart guy when it comes to this type of stuff. It turned out that the guy who they were doing the drop with set the whole thing up.

I found out that Owen visits his brother once every four months in a federal prison in Texas, but he is being moved to a prison in Southern California for his last few months. He said that his brother used to own an auto body shop and owned a house in Westwood until the feds took everything. He told me that his brother had a few things hidden, like his condo.

I was really intrigued by Owen and his family, but at the same time, I was scared of what the future holds for us. I think I love him! His life is so dangerous that he could end up hurt, or worse, but I guess if we are going to be together I have to deal with that. I'm really worried about what could happen! I don't want more pain.

December 26, 1993

I've been so busy with Owen and my schoolwork I have not had time to write in awhile. I don't even have time to write right now 'cause my aunt and I are going to go shopping for all the after-Christmas sales. I had the best Christmas ever! My brother came home for a two-day pass from the rehab place. He looked cool! His face was all clear, and he had put on a little weight. He was real quiet for a little while, but by midnight, when it was time to open the presents, he was laughing and joking with everyone. It was good to see him enjoying himself and back to normal, considering how he was before. I kept thinking about Mom and Dad all Christmas day. Thinking about them made me sad 'cause last Christmas we were together in Arizona as a family. I miss them a lot! I miss Jason a lot too! I was sad to see him leave this morning. I started crying, and when I hugged him good-bye my uncle had to pull us apart. I did not want to let him go. My aunt told me that he will be home in less than a month, on January 20. That really cheered me up! I'll be in school by then. Maybe things will be different for us?

As for me and Owen, things could not be better. We spent Christmas Eve together and exchanged presents. He gave me a gold necklace with half a bear paw on it, and on his necklace was the other half. I was taken aback by that. He told me that we will always be together. I gave him some Obsession cologne. I had no idea what else to get him—he has everything he needs. I did not want to leave him, but I had to because my family was expecting me for dinner that evening. He told me he was going to his uncle's house in L.A. and have Christmas dinner there. I want to see him bad right now. I miss him so much. We are supposed to see each other tomorrow. I can't wait!

December 30, 1993

Last night while I was at Owen's house, I overheard something that scared me! Everything was going fine at first, and then while we were watching a movie, Owen got a distant look on his face and hit the mute button on the TV! I asked him, "What's going on?" and he told me to be quiet and listen. Then I heard what sounded like an earthquake. Owen said, "Damn!" Then he told me to go in the bedroom and don't come out until he comes in to get me. I quickly did what he said because I was really scared.

While I was in the back room I heard three new voices come in the house, and the one they called Dameon was very upset at another guy named Jake. The reason they came over was to ask Owen if he had cut the batch with anything, because some of the clientele had complained and were talking about doing no more business with them. Owen was like, "You know how Jimmy and I do business, Dameon, so I don't even know how you could ask me something like that." After that there was silence, and then Dameon said, "Owen, you know I had to at leasl ask you, before I hit the no-good bastard." Then he laughed and said, "Roll up a few of them joints for us, Owen, and we're out of here!"

After they left, Owen came into the room and got me. I asked him, "What was that about?" He told me that one of the guys who holds the batches after they are made has been stealing dope and replacing it with cut. He was a mask of coolness, as if the events that just transpired were an ordinary occurrence. I, on the other hand, was visibly shaken. I felt very uneasy about the whole situation. As if he was reading my mind, he made a stiff drink of Absolute vodka and cranberry juice, and passed it to me.

After I finished my drink, he talked to me about the days when his brother began transporting for the gang, how scared he used to be when things suddenly happened when he was a kid. He told me about the police raiding his house when he was five years old, and taking his uncle to jail. He said someone was always staying at their house—either on their way somewhere else or hiding from the law. His brother started transporting drugs when he was 16 for their Uncle Joe, who got killed a few years later. Owen was nine at the time! His brother brought him in when he was 14, but all he did was bag up dope and take it to their hiding spot. Owen said that the gang used him for a decoy because he was so young. His Uncle Roy would pick him up from school a few times a week, and one of those times would be the drop. His uncle had a bag in the car identical to the one he took to school, and when he got out of the car he would take that bag and leave his in the car. Then once he got inside he would bag up all the dope in ounces, then crawl under the house and leave it there until morning. Then early in the morning, he would crawl back under the house and grab the bag. Then his brother's girlfriend would be outside waiting to take him to school. She would never come inside!

During the summer, Owen would play baseball, and his uncles, his cousins, their friends, and his brother would come to some of the home games. It all seemed normal, but in actuality, it was a front to do drops. Owen told me that his brother used to give him $200 a week and a half-pound of low-grade marijuana to smoke once a month. Owen told me that his mom would be gone for days at a time, and when she came home she would make Owen give her some money. He said he never wanted to give it to her, but he had to! His brother paid all the bills at Owen's house, and his girlfriend Sheila would buy the groceries for him. He would cook dinner for himself or his mom whenever she ate. Then when Owen was 15 his mom died of an overdose, and his uncle applied for custody of him. The only thing was that nothing changed that much! Owen stayed at his brother's house all by himself, and then his brother went to jail for trafficking dope from California to Nevada and Arizona. The feds took everything he had in his name, and Sheila ran off with what she could. They sold their parents' house to pay for a lawyer, and his brother took a deal for 58 months, but he only has to do 32. A year of his time will be spent in a halfway house. He said his uncle Roy came and gave him a job moving meth locally. He took it because he needed the money to support the family until his brother comes home. I asked him what he meant by that, and he told me that he has to send his brother and father each $500 a month so they can live well prison. He said he is saving money so that when his brother comes home they can open up a business and buy a new house.

We talked a lot about Owen's family until the early hours of the morning, while smoking and drinking. Then we made love and went to sleep. When we woke up, he told me he had to go run some errands, and if I need to go home to just take his Camaro. I took the car home, and it's parked down the street. He also told me that he is going to give me a key to the condo and get me a cell phone. I don't know if I can handle the cell phone because of my uncle. I'm going to tell Owen about my family after we come back from his friends' New Year's party.

[**Note to reader:** *If anything about the person called Owen sounds familiar, please contact us via* www.whathappened2sarah.com.]

January 2, 1994

It's a new year, and I feel better than ever. I start school on Tuesday, and my boyfriend is the coolest man in the world! Today I am going to take pictures. His buddy is going to make me a driver's license so I can have a car. I'm so excited right now everything is going so good. I told Owen about my parents' disappearance last night, and it was very emotional for me. He was very understanding and sympathetic to my situation. When I told him about Ericka's family he was taken aback. His eyes were watery as if he was going to cry, but he is so strong that he did not shed a tear.

It's good to have love in my life again. I feel so complete, so safe, and so secure when I am with him. Just to hear his voice brings unbelievable happiness to my day, and thoughts of him surround my night. I find myself thinking of Owen all throughout the day. It's not thoughts of his face in general. It's

98

thoughts of his smile, his eyes, his cheeks, the way he kisses me, the way he talks to me, the way he holds me, and all my troubles seem to disappear. I'm in love with him.

January 6, 1994

Yesterday was my first day of school! I was a bit uncomfortable, and I felt as if I was going to freak out. The school has two different lunches: first lunch and second lunch. I have first lunch. Jackie has second lunch, so I was all alone during lunch. At first being alone made me feel as if I was odd. No one even attempted to talk to me or make me feel welcome as the new kid in school. I thought of the game Heather and Lindsey used to play—then it hit me! This whole school is grouped up in little cliques. I did not see anyone by themselves and I found that very odd. I quickly went into the library and pretended I was studying so I could make sense of what was going on there. It became apparent that no one was going to talk to me, and no one did. It was the worst first day of school ever.

When I came home, I called Jackie and asked her why she didn't tell me how rude the kids at school are. She told me she did not understand! So I explained everything that happened at school to her. She told me that the kids are not rude, it's that they are just shy like I am. Jackie said all I have to do is talk to one of them and they will open up to me.

When I went to school today I decided to pick someone that I would be compatible with, and I would do it in gym class. I noticed this girl with designer gym clothes that seemed to be the center of attention. I chose her as my target. I walked up to her and said, "Is gym class always like this, or what?" She looked at me, smiled, and said, "It gets worse than this, 'cause Mrs. Bell likes to see you sweat!" From there we began talking, and she told me her name is Judy. It turned out that we both had first lunch together. When I went to lunch, Judy called me over to meet her friends, and I felt accomplished 'cause they're the coolest girls in our class. Judy has an older sister who is a senior, and she is the most popular girl in school. I had a really good day at school today!

Things are not always as bad as they seem. Just when you think that things are not going your way, you get more than you expected out of life. I guess you just have to have faith in yourself! No matter what happens, everything is going to be all right. Well, I have to go meet Owen!

8:00 p.m. Owen is the coolest guy in the world! I can't believe what he did for me. When I got to his house to drop off his car, he was in the parking lot waiting for me, and behind him were two of his friends. He told me to close my eyes and hold out my hand. I did like he told me, and he dropped some keys in my hands. He then told me to open my eyes, and behind him was a beautiful '65 white Mustang convertible. He said, "It's yours, honey! Here's your ID!" He put the car in my name and everything. I was so happy I started crying. I love him so much!

[**Note to reader:** *Sarah was seen by her friends driving a vehicle fitting this description, but nothing was registered in her name.*]

January 8, 1994

I canceled my appointment with Dr. Jones today! I don't feel like I need any more therapy. I told my uncle about it. He told me that if I feel comfortable about my situation, then it's my call. So I don't think I'm going to be going back there anymore.

In three days I have officially become one of the coolest girls in my class. When I pulled up to my school yesterday, everyone was looking at me with their mouths wide open. All the kids at school drive newer-model cars. My car's a classic and plus I have a killer sound system inside. You can hear me for miles. I was playing rap music that the kids at my school have never heard before. Owen knows people in the music business.

I showed Judy my car, and she was like, "That was cool of your parents to give you a car like that!" I told her that my boyfriend gave it to me. She looked at me with the shock of someone who just found out their favorite entertainer died! She said, "Your boyfriend gave you this car?" Then it clicked in my head that I shouldn't tell anyone that. So I told her not to tell anyone about it because he doesn't want everyone to know. She agreed and then asked me how old he is. I told her he is 19 and his parents have a lot of money. Then I changed the subject and told her I don't want to talk about it.

I feel like I messed up because I shouldn't have said that. Owen could get in trouble if people found out that he gave me a car like that. Judy wants to go cruising over to Venice Beach tomorrow. I told her to call me tonight on my cell phone and I'll tell her if it's cool. She was like, "You have a cell phone?" I told her yeah, my parents bought it for me.

Well, I have to meet Owen at some video store right now, so I've got to go.

January 10, 1994

We went over to the beach yesterday. It was cold, so nobody was really out there. Then we went over to Hollywood and I started to feel sick, because it reminded me of Ericka. Jackie, Judy, and Judy's friend Beth were with me. They all wanted to go over to the MGM studios, but Owen called me and he wanted to meet me in a few hours. So we did not have time! I dropped the girls off at Jackie's house and met Owen.

When I got to Owen's house, I called him from the parking lot and he came outside. Then things got all weird, 'cause he seemed stressed out, and when I asked him what was

wrong, he said, "Don't worry about it!" So I knew to back off.
We drove to this shopping center in Glendale, and he handed me
a piece of paper and $100. He told me to go in the store and buy
some things. Then he gave me a kiss and slid some keys in my
pocket.

I went into the little department store and bought some
bath towels, socks, and a clock. At the time, I thought Owen was
coming to pick me up, so I was rushing. Then I remembered the
note. It had an address on it and directions to North Hollywood.
It also told me that there is a Honda Accord in stall number 28
in the parking lot. I bought the stuff, went out to the car, and
left. When I got to the house in North Hollywood, my car was
not there, but I decided to go to the door anyway. I knocked on
the door and a little girl answered. She said, "Are you Sarah?" I
said, "Yes." The little girl handed me some keys with another
note. This note said, go five houses down and get in the green
Jaguar, then go to Jackie's house and wait there.

When I got to Jackie's house, I found it hard to leave the
lush interior and new-car smell of the Jaguar. It must have
taken me at least five minutes to get out of the car. Jackie's
mom knows I drive and she thinks I'm sixteen, but when she saw
me get out of the Jaguar today, she seemed to question my
validity. I'm going to definitely have to park a few houses away
from now on. Her mom never said anything, but the look she

gave me was quite clear—I'm watching you! Maybe I was just high, but even Jackie was like, "You drove a Jag over here?"

After we got settled Jackie told me all about Owen when he was younger. He had all the newest shoes before they came out. His shoes were brand-new every day. He almost never wore the same shoes twice. He always wore outfits that matched and were all by the same designer. When he wore Guess, he was Guess down to his socks. He wore expensive cologne. She said when he turned 15 he was driving a Mercedes to school. All the girls in school wanted to be his girlfriend, but he never dated girls his age. He only dated older girls. She said Owen would drive convertibles during the spring and summer. All of his girlfriends looked like supermodels or movie stars. One of them was a teen TV star.

Before I could finish my talk with her, Owen called and told me he was outside in the driveway. I looked out of the window and there he was, in my Mustang, waiting. So I'm going to get the rest from her tomorrow after school. Owen told me to watch what I say over the phone.

He seems so different from the way Jackie says he used to be. He still dresses nice, but he doesn't seem like the type to hang around movie stars. But I did drive a Jaguar to Jackie's! I wanted to ask him about all that but I decided against it, because he already told me that business we do together we don't discuss. He took me to get something to eat and took me home. He gave me $500 and a few ounces of weed!

January 11, 1994

I cut my third-period class today and got high in the parking lot with Judy. She is pretty cool! I have this feeling of superiority over all the other kids in my class. I feel as if I'm older than they are, because the things they go through seem so childish. Judy was trying to tell me a story about this guy she likes, and I could not find interest in it. I wanted to tell her about the Profile game, but I didn't think it was appropriate.

When she saw the weed we were smoking, she was like, "I have never seen pot like that before!" I told her that it comes from up north and it's high-grade stuff. She was like, "It doesn't even have any seeds!" I started laughing! She was baked all day. Right before school was over she asked me if she could buy some, but I told her I can't sell it, and just gave her some.

She wants to hang out this weekend, but I am going to Tahoe with Owen. I'm so excited, 'cause he just told me about it. Now all I have to do is figure out how to pull this off with my aunt and uncle.

January 13, 1994

I have it all worked out for this weekend! Jackie's going to cover for me, and she even got her mom to help. She is so cool! When I told her where I was going, she was so excited! She wanted to come, but I told her next time. Things are going good!

CHAPTER 5
The Final Entries

January 18, 1994

I don't like this. I thought that Owen and I were going to have more time together in Tahoe, but it was mostly business for him. We barely had any time alone together. I did have fun! I went to the casinos in South Lake Tahoe, and I went snowboarding. I just wish that Owen could have been with me. Paul's girlfriend Janet told me that this is how it is, so get used to it. She was real cool! She is the one who took me around while the boys were doing their thing. The cabin was huge! It was almost as big as Jackie's house. There were five bedrooms, a living room, a family room, and a rumpus room. Janet told me that they have been coming to this cabin for years.

On Saturday night, Owen came into our room with a bag full of money. I've learned to not ask questions and just observe what's going on around me. He looked as if he were under a lot of stress, so I asked him if he wanted a massage or something to eat. That seemed to jolt him, because he stopped doing what he was doing, and looked at me very softly and said, "That would be nice, honey!" I made him a steak and some French fries. He devoured them! Then I gave him a massage, and we made love after that. He opened up to me that night and told me how much he wanted to get out of the business. He said he feels trapped! We talked about his plans for the future. He wants to be a movie director and live on a ranch with horses, cows, and chickens. He looked like a child as he described how he was going to live someday. I wish I could hold on to that night forever. I felt so close to him.

My uncle is mad at me right now because I did not come home until 3:00 this morning, and I was baked out of my mind when I came through the door. He told me that he called Jackie's, and her mom told him that we had gone out with some boys to the skating rink. Then she did not pick up the phone anymore after that. He said he does not want me going out with Jackie anymore, and I can't spend the night at her house anymore. I don't care what he says. I'm going to be with Owen and hang out with Jackie too. He is not my dad. He cannot tell me what to do!

January 20, 1994

Jason came home from rehab this morning, but I didn't get a chance to talk to him yet. I saw him for a brief moment after school as he was on his way out the door with my aunt to go shopping. I was so preoccupied with this party that Owen is throwing, I barely said a word to Jason. I feel bad! It's just that all these people want to come to the party, and I can't let them all come. He told me that only 25 people from my school can come, and everybody is trying to pressure me for a flyer. It's really stressing me out!

January 21, 1994

Jason and I talked for a long time last night! He said that he and Erick used to break into people's houses, even when they were sleeping. They used to go over to Old Man McKinley's house and give him some of the stuff they had stolen for cash. I asked him why he has not told the police, and he said, "'Cause they will kill us!" He had a horrified look in his eyes when he said it. Old Man McKinley has these kids stealing important things like papers, credit cards, checks, driver's licenses, and stuff like that. I wanted to know more, but after a little while he did not want to talk about it so I backed off. I really didn't want to talk about it anymore myself. It reminded me of too many painful things. So truthfully, I was just as happy to change the subject as he was.

I told him about Owen, but I did not tell him the things Owen does. All I told him was that for the first time in a long while I am truly happy. He asked how old Owen was, and I told him a lie. I said Owen was 17. Lucky I did, because Jason was appalled that I was dating someone his age. He was like, what kind of guy wants to date a 15-year-old girl? I took that offensively, but I did not say anything to him. If I had told him that Owen was 19, he would have flipped out! One thing is for sure, our talk opened up my mind to the idea of what Owen sees in me. I mean, he used to date a TV star. I am going to have a talk with him about it!

January 24, 1994

The party was a little wild, but I'm starting to get used to the boys fighting. This fight was a little less violent than the first one was, and it happened in the very beginning, so not that many people were there. It was the other guy's fault. He called Owen a bitch because he couldn't get into the party. They beat him and his friends up pretty bad!

Judy couldn't believe that I'm Owen's girlfriend. When she saw me with Owen, she looked at me with a stunned look on her face and said, "It all makes sense now!" She seemed to have a whole new respect for me, as if I am her idol or something. All the kids I invited treated me like that after they found out I was Owen's girlfriend.

After the party, Owen & I went back to his house and we talked about why he was with someone like me. I told him I could not understand what he sees in me or why he is attracted to me. I began to cry because this is such a wonderful dream that I don't want to wake up from. He held me in his arms and kissed my forehead! When I looked into his eyes, he was crying too! He told me that he fell in love with me the first time he saw me because I looked like his mother. That jolted my heart to skip a beat, sent chills up my spine, and gave me the stiffest goose bumps I've ever had. He stood up, reached in his back pocket, pulled out his wallet, and showed me her picture. I look just like her!

January 26, 1994

The freaking school called today and told my aunt that I cut yesterday. My uncle came home and told me that I'm grounded. He said no telephone calls in or out, and if I cut again he is sending me to a boarding school. I love my uncle and aunt very much, but nothing is going to stop me from seeing or talking to Owen. Nothing!

January 28, 1994

I left my cell phone at home, and my aunt found it. My uncle was yelling about where did I get a cell phone, who was paying for it, and a whole bunch of other stuff. He busted up my phone with a hammer! I'm out of here and I'm not coming back. Fuck them! I have Owen. He welcomed me to move in with open arms. I'm so happy.

January 31, 1994

Jackie called over here today and said my uncle is looking for me. She said he called the police and he filed a missing persons report. I told her I don't think that I'm going to school anymore, because the police are going to try and pick me up. I'm not leaving Owen!

[**Note to reader**: *A missing person's report was filed by Sarah's uncle in accordance with the timeline of these dates.*]

February 15, 1994

Valentine's Day was almost totally ruined! Owen's friend went to jail and Owen spent almost the whole day running around doing errands to cover his friend's affairs. Then he had me go down to the bail bonds with a fake ID and bail him out. I thought that the whole day was a loss. When I got home, Owen had Chinese food for me, with flowers, balloons, and a teddy bear. It was so cute because he had candles lit and everything. Then after we finished eating, we watched a movie while eating chocolate-covered strawberries, whipped cream, and champagne. He is so wonderful! I love my valentine.

February 18, 1994

Owen left for Mexico this morning. He is not coming back for at least two days. I wanted to go with him so badly, but he is working on a big deal so I can't come. He is really excited

112

about this because he said it's his exit out of the business. I hope everything goes all right. I miss him so much!

February 21, 1994

Jackie stayed over for the weekend and kept me company, but all I did was think about Owen. He still hasn't come back, and he hasn't called. This is driving me crazy, and I do not know what to do to calm myself down.

February 22, 1994

Owen came back last night, and he went right back out. He looked irritated, so I did not ask him how things went. All he said to me was, "Hi, honey! I'll be back." He grabbed some money out of the safe and changed cars. He still has not come back!

February 23, 1994

Owen came home last night and he looked so worn out. His eyes were bloodshot and his clothes were wrinkled up. He said he just came back from Mexico again and everything is fine now. He passed out and left early this morning again. I need to find something to occupy my time during the day, because all I do is worry about him.

February 25, 1994

Owen just left and told me to pack up all my things, because we have to move. I asked him why, and he said he will tell me later. Then he left. He said that he will be back in two hours, so be ready to go. I'm scared! I wonder what's going on. He had this frantic look on his face as if his thoughts were on a million other things. Well, I've got to get packed up!

February 27, 1994

This place is really nice! I can't believe that this house is Owen's. I don't understand why we never came here before. I mean he told me that he doesn't stay here a lot because he does so much business that it might raise suspicion. I feel like a princess or something 'cause other girls my age still live with their parents. My boyfriend has a house in the Chino Hills! It's not in his name, he says, but I could care less. I'm going to go get Jackie and bring her over here to my new house!

March 1, 1994

Owen yelled at me and called me stupid, because I told Jackie that this is his house. I didn't know I shouldn't say anything to Jackie. He just looked at me and gave me a cold stare that I have never seen in his eyes before. Then he told me that I am stupid and stormed out of the house. I kept telling him how sorry I was, but he didn't want to hear it. He told me that one slip and this whole thing is history. I feel so stupid right now, because I should have known not to talk about what Owen does, but it's just that Jackie asked how much this place cost, and now everything is ruined. He is going to break up with me and never talk to me again. Why does everything good in my life have to be taken away from me? I don't want to lose him! I hate myself.

March 2, 1994

Owen did not come home last night, and he did not answer his cell phone. I don't know what to think! I thought he would have at least come home this morning, but it's evening and he is still not home. What have I done? I have no one I can talk to about this, because I don't want to make him mad. What am I going to do?

March 3, 1994

Owen came home at 3:00 this morning, and he was in some clothes I've never seen before. I tried to talk to him, but he did not want to talk. All he wanted to do was have sex. I let him because I'll do anything for him. Then this morning when I woke up he was gone. I guess he is not really that upset about me telling Jackie about the house, and he is not going to break up with me. I just wonder where he stays when he is gone. I know he has other places to stay. It's just that I don't like sleeping by myself. I miss him!

March 4, 1994

Owen and I talked last night about the business. He told me that his brother is coming home in less than a month and that things are going to change when he gets out. I asked him how. He just said he did not know exactly, but things are definitely going to change!

I thought he would be excited about his brother coming home, but he seemed stressed out about it. It was almost as if he didn't want him to come home at all. He told me that the thing he just put together in Mexico is going to make it so he only has to touch the stuff twice a year. He said all he will see is the money mostly, and he is opening up an auto body shop with his uncle. I am so worried about him because he seems stressed out all the time, and things that should bring him happiness only bring him more worry. I wish I could take his pain away.

March 6, 1994

Owen took me to his shop yesterday. When he told me that he was opening up an auto body shop, I thought it would take a little while. They are opening on Tuesday! I met his uncle Pooh Bear. I thought that name fit him perfectly, 'cause he is a big guy who looks like a teddy bear. They already had cars inside that the guys were working on. Owen asked me to answer the phones and do the paperwork until they find someone permanent. I finally feel as if I'm needed. I'm so happy to be able to do something for him. His birthday is this month on the 27th, and his uncle said we are going to throw a party for him. I'm so excited!

March 8, 1994

I just got back from work! It was very busy for their first day of business, the place was packed with customers all day. Seemed like when one person was coming out, another was coming in. We are backed with orders until June. Uncle Pooh was turning people away by the middle of the day. The strange thing is that Uncle Pooh knew almost all of the customers, and the ones he didn't know knew Dave the mechanic. They are so busy that they are working the body guys even on graveyard shift for pay under the table.

Owen came to work for about two hours in the morning just to have a meeting with some paint dealers, and then he was gone all day. He is still not home, but that's the way things have to be, I guess! I'm going to make dinner just in case he is hungry when he gets home. He's not answering his phone!

March 10, 1994

I just can't believe what I just saw! This has got to be some kind of joke or freaking hallucination, 'cause I did not see what I just saw! It's been awhile since I had seen or heard from Jackie, so I decided to just swing by after work and surprise her. I parked a little down the street, because I didn't want her mom to see the new Acura that Owen gave me. I was just about to go up to her driveway when I saw her getting out of Owen's Mercedes. She leaned over and kissed him! This cannot be happening to me—my best friend and my boyfriend?

I don't know what to do about this, 'cause I don't want to lose Owen. I know what I'm going to do. I'm going to call Jackie and tell her I want to hang out for awhile tomorrow. Then I'm going to confront that bitch about messing around with my boyfriend! All I know is she better leave him alone or I'm going to whoop her ass.

March 12, 1994

God, I wanted it to be a dream so bad, but I called her house and her mom said she is not home yet. She never came home from school yesterday and she hasn't called, which is not like her, her mom said. She told me if I heard from her, to tell her to call home.

I'm so scared right now! I should have told her mom what happened, but she would never have believed me. No one would believe me! I just hope that she is all right and nothing bad has happened to her. I must write down what happened just in case in the future someone reads this and I'm gone, 'cause it might help explain some things. If I hadn't tried to scare her, she would be at home right now. I'm so stupid to think that it was all over!

I told Jackie to meet me at the frozen yogurt place at 6:00 p.m., and don't tell anyone who she's going to see because Owen will trip! She was there on time and by herself. I never got out of the car. I just honked the horn and she got in. She began to compliment the new car Owen had gotten for me, and told me how lucky I was to have a boyfriend like that. Her fake words brought anger to me, but I kept my cool by firing up some pot.

I began some small talk about how I was unhappy with my life just to see what she would say. She was silent for quite some time. I had already decided to take her around the hills of Hollywood, before I would change the conversation to what I had seen. I pulled over into an abandoned driveway to what appeared to be an old shed. When I told her what I had seen, she began to cry. She told me how sorry she was. I told her to get out of my car, 'cause I was leaving her there. She would not get out! So I reached over, opened her door, and tried to push her out.

That's when I saw two men on her side of the door. They reached in and grabbed her out. When I screamed, one of them bent down and said, "How you been, honey? We missed you. Tell Jason we said hello." It was Erick, and Alex was with him! I just backed out of there with the door open and everything!

I can't believe I drove to the exact same spot where Erick had taken me before! Maybe it wasn't the same spot, but it had to be, because they couldn't have followed us. I wonder if they know where I live. This sounds like a bunch of bullshit, but it's the honest to god's truth. I hope they let her go! How am I'm going to tell Owen about this?

[**Note to reader**: *Authorities believe something in this entry speaks to the events in the still open murder case of Jackie Keller. Jackie's mother confirms that she has never met the person referred to as "Owen," as noted in Sarah's diary entries.*]

March 13, 1994

I feel so sick to my stomach! I had a dream about Jackie, and I was so happy that she was all right. Then I woke up and my living nightmare continued. I can't believe I left her, but I was so scared, it was just a reflex. I thought Erick and Alex were long gone from my life. They were so far from my mind that the sight of them brought pure shock and horror to my heart all over again. Just thinking about them right now grips me with an unbelievable terror that I can't explain. It's like waking up in a coffin or something, 'cause there is no way out and I can't explain how I got here.

Owen asked me if I had heard from Jackie this morning. I felt a sense of anger that he was inquiring about her, and for a brief moment today, I was glad she was gone. I hate myself for feeling like that about her, because it was just as much his fault as hers. I know now that I cannot tell Owen about what happened, because he will never believe me. This is another secret I'm going to have to hold with me forever.

March 15, 1994

My conscience is bothering me to the point of no return. I had to call Jackie's mom today and find out if she has heard anything yet. She told me the police are on it, but so far nothing has come about. I told her to keep me posted on the latest developments, because I'm really worried about her. Then her mom started crying, which made me cry, and I hurried to get off the phone. It hurts me to know that it's all my fault that she is not home, and possibly could never come home. I wish there was something I could do to take away this pain.

Owen has been home every night since she disappeared! Looking at him makes me sick, because he was sleeping with her, and now that she is gone, he stays home. He wanted to have sex last night. I told him I couldn't because

Jackie being missing hurts me, and I just don't feel in the mood. He is mad at me, and I could care less. This is all his fault!

March 19, 1994

They found Jackie in the hills last night! She is dead! What am I going to do? I have to do something. I was at Jackie's house talking to her mother when the police came over with the news. We all were hoping on the way down to the county coroner's that it wasn't going to be her, but when I heard the scream from her mother, all my hopes were crushed inside of her cries. When her mother finally came out of the room, she looked as if she had aged 20 years in a matter of minutes. Her pain and devastation seemed to fill every room that she walked in, leaving whoever was in the room intoxicated in her wake. I had no words, only tears, and when I finally spoke, the only thing I could say was "Sorry." The air was so thick with the smell of death, pain, and loss that it almost seemed to choke my cries. It was an all-too-familiar smell to me now, and I knew it well. Before my parents died, I never had paid attention to it. Now I recognize it as if it were a designer fragrance.

When I told Owen about Jackie, he was in shock for a brief moment, and for quite some time he was speechless. His shock quickly turned to rage. He was unrecognizable to me, 'cause I had never witnessed this side of him. It hurt me a great deal, because I knew that he loved her. He was yelling things like "Whoever did this is going to pay!" I barely paid attention to it because I was so busy crying over the fact that he loved her so much. I was in a daze, because when I looked up, Owen was gone! For a while I thought that he was still in the house, but I soon learned he had left altogether. That was a few hours ago, and he is not answering his phone. He really loved her!

March 21, 1994

Jackie's funeral is this Saturday, and the memorial service is Friday night. I think I am not going to go the funeral because it's going to be painful. Why should I go? To say goodbye to my friend? I don't want to hear people who talk about where she is and who she was. I want to remember her laughing, fun-loving, preppy self, and pretend that she is still on this planet, but I just can't reach her anymore. That's the way I want to think of my friend. Owen thinks it's wrong not to pay my respects by going to the funeral. We got into a big fight last night about it, 'cause he can't understand the way I feel when it comes to death. Especially when I am responsible, but I cannot tell him that, so he is in a void when it comes to the full explanation of my reasoning. How can I look at Jackie and watch her family mourn when she would still be alive had I not done what I did? I can't do that, 'cause it will destroy me. I just can't!

March 22, 1994

Owen's making me go to the funeral to pay my respects to his girlfriend.

March 24, 1994

While I was out shopping today, I think I saw Ericka! The mall was not that crowded this afternoon, so I decided to go buy some clothes for the memorial service. When I got there I was so hungry that I could not go shopping until I ate. So I went to the food court. I sat down and began eating. I can't explain why, but I felt the need to look up, and that's when I saw her. She was standing by the entrance to the food area, just staring at me, and when I looked at her she continued to stare. It was as if she was a mannequin until she smiled at me. I was frozen with fear that made the hair on the back of my neck stand up, and I was forced to look away. When I looked up, she was gone! The greatest sense of relief seemed to engulf my body.

I put it out of my mind and began shopping, but the paranoia seemed to have me on edge. I could not fully relax and focus on what I was looking for, 'cause I knew she was somewhere around. I could feel her! Was it a ghost? Could I have just

124

imagined the whole thing? I don't know what to think, but all I know is I saw her and she is dead. I mean, yeah, it could have been someone who looked like her, but if it was, then why was she staring at me like she was, and then smiling? That's too much of a coincidence for it to be a complete stranger. I guess I'm just under a lot of stress and I probably took a perfect stranger's actions the wrong way. That's got to be it. I need to take a bath and relax. It couldn't have been Ericka.

March 27, 1994

Owen didn't want a party. We sat at home and watched movies. He's acting so different. I wonder how long they were together.

March 28, 1994

The funeral was traumatic! Jackie's mom threw herself onto the casket when the pallbearers closed it. She let out a sound that I have never heard before in my life. It was a cross between a seagull and a donkey with a touch of hyena. The sound still echoes in my ears. I was so happy when everything was over, but the images will continue to haunt me. It seemed as if everyone in the room knew that I was responsible, because their eyes seemed to show anger whenever I caught them glancing in my direction. What have I done? I'm a monster!

This is all Owen's fault! I wouldn't have even gone to the funeral had it not been for him. He insisted that I go and pay my respects to her family. Some respect I showed by coming. All I did was watch all the pain and hurt that I caused an entire family to suffer. Now I'm haunted forever!

April 3, 1994

Owen's brother Jimmy is home! They both walked into the shop yesterday and the family resemblance is so great that I instantly knew who he was. Jimmy's eyes are cold and piercing. He has the kind of stare that makes you look away, but his charm and charisma are very appealing. They were only there briefly and then they were gone celebrating Jimmy's release from prison. I wonder what's in store for us now.

April 6, 1994

Owen is so happy to have his brother back home. I thought that once Jimmy came home, Owen would be home more, but it seems like he is home less now. I know it has not been that long since he came home, but I guess I expected it to be an instant thing. One thing is for sure: when it comes to who is in charge, Jimmy is definitely in control. When he came into the shop today, he was directing people left and right. Hell, it seemed like people wouldn't even take a crap unless they talked to him first. I'm not too happy about what is going on here, and I hope that things change soon.

April 9, 1994 - Crazy

Somebody followed me home tonight. I don't know who or what is driving me crazy, but someone is trying to get me. I wasn't even paying attention to what was going on, and Owen always told me to watch out because people might try to hurt me to get to him. I feel so stupid, because all I was thinking about was what they are doing at the shop, and not thinking about what's going on around me. I was just so upset to find out that they are turning stolen cars into used cars. I overheard Uncle Pooh talking about he needs four Mercedes by next weekend for a client. Then he said, "Make sure to change all of the VIN numbers this time." It was just so much to take in that I could not think of anything else.

The street we live on is a private cul-de-sac, and there is very little traffic that comes our way. I noticed when I got on our street that a car had been behind me for quite some time. When I pulled into the driveway, they turned in behind me and turned their bright lights on. My heart skipped a beat, and I was frozen with fear. Then they pulled out of the driveway and honked the horn. I could not see exactly what kind of car it was, but it was definitely a truck. I wonder what that was all about. When Owen comes home I am going to tell him about it.

April 11, 1994

I have got to tell Owen what's going on, but it's never the right time. I don't want to sound crazy by telling him only bits and pieces, 'cause he won't take me seriously. I can't tell him the entire story, because he is going to think I'm crazy. What am I going to do? Somebody called and said, "We miss you," and hung up the phone. It was a woman's voice that sounded so similar to Ericka's that it was chilling. I must have stood there frozen with the phone in my hand for a minute or two. When I hung it up I had to back away from it. The hand that had held the receiver was shaking and tingling like it had electrified me.

That was last night! Tonight when I went outside to grab the letters I forgot to mail in the car, there was a white rose on the doormat. I quickly closed the door and locked it. When Owen came home I asked him if he saw the roses on the doormat. He looked at me like I was crazy and said, "What are you talking about?" So we went to the door together and the rose was gone. I was so stunned and I felt so stupid 'cause Owen laughed and said, "Stay off the drink, baby." Then he left again. I'm so scared to be home alone right now. The wind is blowing softly, but I hear this scratching noise every now and then coming from the side of the house. I'm in the bedroom with the door locked with Owen's gun right next to me. I'm so scared. Oh my God, someone is in the house!

April 12, 1994

I have got to get out of here! I don't want to leave Owen, 'cause I love him so much, but if I don't leave they are going to kill me. I have to go somewhere safe. I wish I could find Heather, 'cause she is the only one who understands what's going on. I just can't believe what happened today. I'm at work, which is the only place I have left where I feel safe, and Jimmy walked through the door with Alex following behind him. My eyes filled up with tears of horror and I let out a scream from deep within my body. I startled everyone including myself. I jumped up and ran to the corner of the office and passed out. When I woke up I was on the couch in Uncle Pooh's office. Owen was there and he was asking me if I felt all right, and the fear came back into me. I told Owen that Jimmy's friend is trying to kill me—he killed my parents and two of my friends. Owen looked at me as if he was confused and told me Jimmy came in here by himself. I tried to tell him that there was someone behind him, but it was no use. The verdict was in, and I am crazy!

I know what I saw and I have to leave here soon, because it's too dangerous. I'm going to sit down and have a talk with Owen before I go. I have to talk with my brother and find out what they want with me. I'm going to tell Owen everything from the beginning so he can understand what I'm going through. I've already called my uncle, and we talked for a long time. He said I am more than welcome back home and everyone will be happy to see me. I hate that I have to leave Owen, but it's for the best.

April 13, 1994

It feels good to be back home! My aunt was crying when I walked through the door, and she embraced me so tightly with the energy from her love that I started crying too. My uncle had a look of complete shock on his face because of my appearance. He told me that I looked like I had grown up 10 years. He said I no longer looked like a little girl, but a young woman. We all sat and talked for quite some time, and then Jason came home. He was not as happy to see me as I expected. He greeted me as one would greet someone they see every day— no hugs, no how are you doing, no it's good to see you—just, "Hi, Sarah," and he quickly ran upstairs. My uncle told me that Jason is working at a golf course as a caddie-attendant, and that he has a girlfriend he met a few months back. I wanted to talk with Jason, but he was out the door as quickly as he arrived.

When I went to sleep last night, I cried because Owen wasn't there in bed with me. I went to the phone and called him. He told me that he would come by and see me after work. I'm still waiting for him. He hasn't picked up his phone, and Uncle Pooh said he left over two hours ago. I guess he is just busy and got caught up with some other things. I guess our relationship is going to be changing a bit.

April 14, 1994

Jason scared me last night! He came into my room while I was sleeping and was just standing over me. I lay still, frozen with fear, because when I said his name he did not reply. He just turned around and whispered, "You shouldn't have come back!" Then he walked out of the room. I was too terrified to go back to sleep. I fought sleep all night and finally gave in when the sun came up. When I woke up I thought I had dreamed the whole thing, so I went into Jason's room. He was not there! I don't know if it was real or not, 'cause I may have just been dreaming. Why would I dream of fighting sleep? I don't want to tell my aunt and uncle because I just got here. Plus, they are so proud of Jason's recovery that I would sound like a trouble-maker.

Owen never showed up yesterday, and he's not picking up his phone. I called Uncle Pooh and he said Owen was not there yet, but he should be in later today. I think I'm going to go over to his house and surprise him. I still have the key, so I'll just wait for him.

[**Note to reader**: *The following events are in great question because authorities cannot match a crime scene within a hundred mile radius to the events mentioned in Sarah's April 15, 1994 entry. Please read the following entries carefully.*]

April 15, 1994

Why? Oh my god, why? This cannot be happening to me. What the hell do they want from me? They took the last thing I had left on this earth that I truly loved. We went to the end of time together, then held each other and cried, 'cause there was nowhere else to go but back! My darling Owen, why did they take you away from me? This has got to be a nightmare and I'm going to wake up soon. I can still feel his warm body pressed against me as we made love last night. I can still smell him and taste him. When I reached over for him this morning, my hand touched something slimy, and when I looked at my hand, warm blood dripped off it. I looked over at my beloved Owen, and he was cut into some unrecognizable monster. He was dead! How did it happen? He must have struggled, but I did not wake up. I wanted to call the police, but they would not believe me. How could I sleep through something like that? I just left.

I wish I could wake up and have him lying next to me. I wish I could wake up from this terrible nightmare. How can Owen be gone? I have to go!

April 16, 1994

Jason came into my room last night again and said, "When you see Owen, tell him I said hello." My eyes filled up with tears, and when I looked, he was gone. I sat there for a minute and then got up because my fear had turned into anger. When I went his room, he was gone. I'm staying up all night until I can talk to him, 'cause if he knows anything about Owen being murdered, he is going to tell me tonight.

April 17, 1994 – Last Entry

When I reach the sunset to cross the night, I will be with the ones I loved in life. Everyone I love is now gone, and I am all alone. I'm leaving this book so that all will hear my tale, and know I have no home. I woke up again to find no life around me—only empty bodies. My brother, my aunt, and my uncle. Ericka woke me up before she left and told me that I will always be welcome in her home. With that she laughed and ran off. I screamed for my uncle, but he did not come. I ran to his room, and the door was open. My uncle and aunt lay there dead! When I went to Jason's room, he was also dead. It is an all-too-familiar scene, and one that I must say I'm used to. No tears to cry, 'cause I have no more left. As you read my story, understand that it is a tale about a girl who lost everyone she ever loved. If you ever see me wandering the streets, please excuse me if I do not speak. I'm doing you a favor by staying away, because befriending me could mean your last day.

AFTERWORD

There was a nationwide search for Sarah, but the search ended when the badly burned remains of a young woman were found. For many years the police assumed that the deceased woman was Sarah Brown because a bracelet found on the remains matched one Sarah was known to wear. However, recently the remains were exhumed for DNA testing at the request of Sarah's family. The test results did not match the family's DNA, further substantiating the family's belief that Sarah is still out there.

Over the years since Sarah went missing, family members have received strange phone calls from a woman who sounds similar to Sarah; but the caller has never identified herself. There have also been sightings by family members in Arizona of a young woman who looks similar to Sarah; however, contact has never been made with the individual.

After reading her diary and examining the facts of the case, many unanswered questions continue to puzzle the family. Some believe that Sarah was responsible for all of the murders and that the characters who chased her throughout the spree were alter egos.

Except for the victims, none of the people mentioned by Sarah in her diary seem to have existed; it's as if she made them up. The first victim, Ericka Lane, did not fit the description of the wild and crazy girl depicted in Sarah's accounts. One thing is certain: Sarah couldn't have killed Ericka Lane, because she was already dead when she and Sarah supposedly met.

Others believe that Sarah is telling the truth. They think she was pulled into an occult world and has spent many years in hiding from those people. They believe that the young woman who called herself Ericka was a participant in this cult and was the catalyst in this formula for murder.

www.ingramcontent.com/pod-product-compliance
Lightning Source LLC
Chambersburg PA
CBHW020345260626
47156CB00004B/1687